Zig Zag

Lucy Robertson

BLACK SWAN

ZIG ZAG
A BLACK SWAN BOOK   0 552 99483 9

Published simultaneously in hardcover by Doubleday,
a division of Transworld Publishers Ltd

PRINTING HISTORY
Black Swan edition published 1992

This book is set in 11/12pt Melior by
County Typesetters, Margate, Kent

Black Swan Books are published by Transworld
Publishers Ltd., 61–63 Uxbridge Road, Ealing, London
W5 5SA, in Australia by Transworld Publishers (Australia)
Pty. Ltd., 15–23 Helles Avenue, Moorebank, NSW 2170,
and in New Zealand by Transworld Publishers (N.Z.) Ltd.,
3 William Pickering Drive, Albany, Auckland.

Made and printed in Great Britain by
Cox & Wyman, Reading, Berks.

Lucy Robertson was born in Cornwall.
She taught in a Harambee school in
Kenya before reading Biochemistry at
London University. She has also worked
in Sierra Leone and Panama. She
obtained a PhD in Parasitology at
Glasgow University, and is working as a
research parasitologist in Scotland.

Author photograph by A. T. Campbell

For m, d & b

Chapter One

July 30th 1964 and a wedding: one of those cloying weddings of sugared almonds and confetti. There were gold-paper doilys, a glitter of cut glass and silver plate, and swathes of drapery in pastel shades that drooped like wilted lettuce leaves. One of those weddings where the superficial, chattering bonhomie went just deep enough for the peachy, rag-tag bunch of hangers-on, only invited through accident or carelessness or because of whom they've married, to be unaware of the swirling, curling, vicious currents that pushed and thrust amongst the smiling throng.

At the top table, flouncily and ridiculously arrayed as bridesmaid to Ziggy and Arabella, I could scan and view the unaware faces, glowing pink, smiling and chewing their way through rack of lamb and strawberry Eton mess. Vacuous talk with quickly forgotten strangers and all the easy pleasure of a free meal and another pair launched into the meteor-strewn orbit of matrimonial bliss. Arabella sat straight-backed and haughtily beautiful, and Ziggy shone and strutted with pride and pleasure, and most of all, with a furious, blazing triumph. Only the nearest or dearest would have any inkling of previous chapters, and who was near or dear anyway?

'Close to the throne,' thought I, and then smiled, or more probably smirked. I was watching Mother, demented and incontinent, wriggling fretfully on the commode that the hotel staff had been begged, and bribed (I saw money changing hands), to bring to the top table.

Marsdon, fat and as glaringly white as a suet pudding, also sat uncomfortably, rolled into too-tight shiny trousers and an ill-fitting jacket. He had been bullied and battered by Ziggy into being best man, and I felt no pity or remorse for the imminent humiliation of a speech that I knew would be dogged by his stammer, his buck teeth and his merciless lack of wit, originality or invention. Ziggy had not wanted me to be waltzed out of the church behind him, to the clash of bells and the unforgiving eye of the photographer, by somebody that I might care to be with or be seen with. Yet it was solid, greasy Marsdon, pores wide and steaming, who suggested in his best man's speech, witty as an ancient flaccid dumpling on a damp Wednesday afternoon and the smell of stale dog-piss outside a Methodist chapel, that the romance of Ziggy and Arabella might one day be written down.

How many years ago was that now? Ten or twenty, or maybe one hundred and twenty. Does it even matter? Now, on the train to London, drumming north through Exeter, I can think back on Marsdon's words as though they were stuttered yesterday. It is but two days now since Marsdon, perceiving his life as valueless, wrote words whose pathos makes you squirm rather than weep, and hung himself from a coat peg by the cord of his blue towelling dressing gown; the shower-curtain rail had apparently been his first attempt, but had broken under his weight before the deed was completed.

Perhaps his perceptions were not entirely hopeless, for as I chug towards the witnessing of his reduction to a so much more elegant urn of ashes, I can see that there is only one person who can write the tale of Ziggy and Arabella, and if Marsdon hadn't suggested it, perhaps I would never have bothered.

Chapter Two

I have known Ziggy, as Sigmund has always been called, either for as long as I can remember, and longer, or I have never known him at all. Whichever way it is, he is my only brother, or, at least, the only one I know of, and he was there when I was born.

It was, by any standards, a birth which one could describe as awkward. A home delivery in rural Cornwall in a November characterized by a malicious and persistent frost and ice that decapitated the Dracena palms and froze solid the locks on the midwife's car. My father, in duffle coat and knitted brown wool gloves, finally slithered and slewed the four or so miles to the stranded midwife on an ancient bald-tyred bicycle to solve her dilemma with a little imagination and a pint of hot water. By the time they had returned I was born, ugly and wrinkled as new babies are, and the saucepan in which my father had been sterilizing string for tying the umbilical cord had boiled dry, filling the air with acrid fumes. Three-year-old Ziggy, robustly plump and rather solemn, was trying to silence my mother's screams by sitting on her face with a pillow, and perhaps he was not too far from success. Whether the dementia and incontinence really began there is hard to guess. Ziggy, for one, has never doubted it.

The usefulness and experience of the midwife is questionable. Although she presumably tidied up any excess of gore and told my father I was a girl, history suggests that a large proportion of her work involved having her spirits fortified by accepting my father's celebratory offerings of salty roll-mop herrings and several substantial tumblers of a very fine ruby port that had been bought in anticipation of Christmas. These tales of drunken carelessness and frivolity inevitably have a moral or cautionary ending. As she drove homewards, the midwife ploughed into a telegraph pole or lamp-post at considerable speed, and if a broken neck is a rapid death, then so was hers.

The crash of metal on metal came grating through the still, frosted night, the haze of port and my mother's whimpers, and brought my father quickly to the scene. He was in his wellington boots, pyjamas and dressing gown, for he had been on his way to bed, but he left those brown wool knitted gloves at home. The next morning, amputation was the answer for the tips of three fingers of his right hand, blackened by frostbite as he'd wrestled to open the midwife's car door, frozen closed again. It was certainly not a propitious arrival into the world, and the burden of blame that Ziggy rested on my one-day-old shoulders was not a small one.

If I had arrived in the world with a bang, I was now going to spend a good few years whimpering. My hapless parents spent the first few weeks of my life in the local hospital in the tiny misty cathedral city of Trelvo, about fifteen miles from their home. My father had developed a bubbling, racking pneumonia from his wrestling in the chill birthday-night air. It apparently matched the misery of his frostbite and it rendered him useless as a source of comfort for both his baby daughter and for the pitiful mother of his baby daughter. The midwife's husband was seeking legal retribution from my father for plying his unfortunate wife with such copious amounts of alcohol, and although it seems obvious now that he was fighting a hopeless battle, he was another awkward factor in the whole miserable turmoil. Yes, Christmas spirit was at a low ebb that year, and Ziggy and I were placed in the care of a venomous spinster whom I was later to learn to call Aunt Bernice.

Aunt Bernice, who was not a blood relation, was as wrinkled and tough as a dried apricot. Her breath smelt fetid and decayed, and when she spoke, which was rarely, for she was miserly with expression, her words also seemed twisted with a rank sourness. Why two small children, one of whom was no more than a newly-born squalling baby, hungry and fractious, should have been entrusted to her care, is a question that I have often pondered upon. It is a matter as mysterious as the size of the universe, and the answer is even less likely ever to be resolved. Nevertheless, not only did I spend my first milky, wailing Christmas in her charge, not only were Ziggy and I condemned to her care for the following fifteen years, but also, a mere five days after the arrival of my greedy, querulous presence, Aunt Bernice took it upon herself to choose a name for me.

It is a fact, and one that has never been denied or questioned, even by those few who knew her best, that Aunt Bernice was singularly devoid of even the slightest trace of sense of humour, subtle or otherwise. It can, therefore, only be put down to sheer perversity and malice that she chose to plant upon my helpless self the obscure, indeed, as far as I know, the hitherto unheard-of, name of Zag. Whether my father was so absorbed in his own problems, and my mother already beyond the scope of capable and rational thought, that they were incapable of defending their baby daughter against the imposition of this name, is yet another of those mysteries of my early childhood. If any protest was raised, then it was raised too late to avoid the harsh black and white evidence of the birth certificate, and too late to delay the first faltering, lisping attempts of Ziggy to put a name to the rumple-faced small monster that he so clearly associated with the disruption and dismay that had fallen across his own life.

11

*   *   *

The spirit of New Year is a curious phenomenon. Following rapidly on the bloated excesses of Christmas, the beginning of January is a time of new resolves and vapid sentiments, all declared through a haze of whisky fumes and cigarette smoke. False cheers and false tears for false friends are unleashed to the telling toll of the midnight strike. A new year begins, but how often does this mark the beginning of anything else, despite the resolutions?

Of course, at two months old, 1 January washed past me regardless. Aunt Bernice would have driven any spirits to malevolence anyway. Nevertheless, changes were occurring, and new starts were implemented at this time. By 2 January, my mother had settled into some sort of helpless, hopeless routine. She was discharged from the soft grey hospital at Trelvo, and readmitted into a long-term nursing home of stern red brick and brisk efficiency at Bodwell. Here, young, strong nurses smelling of carbolic soap and the knowledge of intimate secrets, could constrict her limbs when they flailed too wildly and, unlucky them, change her ever-filling nappies. She cannot have been a difficult patient to handle then, for she was as tiny and frail as a wasted sparrow, although in later life she acquired surprising rolling waves of bulbous flab, but constraining the flutters of her excited wings must have been wearisome. Nursing is truly a noble profession, and can only be mastered by saints and idiots.

Two days later, 4 January, my father set out for East Africa, and out of our lives. The midwife's husband had diminished to no more than a toothachy, querulous, nagging trouble from his previous position as an ominous threat; my mother was in those clean capable hands of the Bodwell nurses; we children were in the crotchety, crabbed claws of Aunt Bernice. For my father to choose this time to accept a long-standing offer of some big-game shooting safaris from an old

12

friend, manager of a tea plantation in the lush, red-soiled highlands of Kenya, can only have been escapism.

Before he left, he added some curious codicils to his will 'just in case . . .' To Ziggy he left an aged box of lead soldiers, their legs crumpled beneath them from their own weight, and his gold fountain pen with a chipped nib. To me he merely wanted to leave those brown wool gloves, so closely associated with my disastrous arrival in the world. I have those gloves beside me now; they are the only part of my father that I know at all well. The wool has bobbled and snagged. At the tips of the fingers they have become felted and matted and they are pervaded with the fruity, leafy scent of pipe tobacco. If these gloves were left to me that I might be able in some way to conjure up a ghostly image of my father, then they have failed. The pictures that they create in my mind of a smoking, bearded, swashbuckling rascal, are at variance with all the photographic evidence. My father was short, stout, clean-shaven and rather prim. He never smoked a pipe, or, I am told, anything else; Aunt Bernice had stored those gloves for me in a discarded tobacco tin. I feel it should be that those gloves tell a story, but, alas, the tales that they whisper to me are lies.

My father was never meant for tropical life. Quirks in his fastidious nature should have warned him. Three weeks into his stay in Kenya, thrusting his plump white-stockinged left leg into the high riding boots that he had left overnight on the veranda, he was bitten on the arch of his foot by a lithe nestling boomslang. Boomslangs are beautiful snakes, the brightest, wildest green imaginable, but they are bad-tempered brutes too, and there is a high price to be paid for being bitten. Within days, or more probably weeks, for to a baby or child days and weeks are an indistinct blur, the brown woollen gloves were incarcerated in the tobacco tin. Due to my mother's frail

13

mental and physical condition and further codicils written in my father's will, written through a hurried and foolish ignorance I believe now, although I confess I have thought it could only have been a vindictive spitefulness, Aunt Bernice was to be the legal guardian of both Ziggy and myself until Ziggy reached his eighteenth birthday.

Chapter Three

The house of my childhood is tall and dark in the shadows of my memories. The windows were small and the woodwork was painted a heavy brown. There were three floors and an attic, all connected by steep narrow staircases with stern olive-green carpets worn thin at the corners and on the treads. The rooms were cluttered with large ungainly pieces of agelessly old furniture. There were several heavy leather-covered armchairs stuffed with horsehair and draped with greasy antimacassars, and most of the narrow, cluttered rooms were burdened with ponderous, dark wood sideboards pushed hard against the walls, with rust-freckled mirrors and empty drawers that stuck half-open when you peeked inside them, hoping for a lost treasure, but never finding one. Even the brightest summer sunshine that attempted to slant through the windows became faded as it was absorbed in the dusty gloom of the lost, frightened corners amongst the furniture legs.

The back garden was small, the grass permanently rank and yellowing in the shade of an overgrown fuchsia hedge which seemed to be always dank and abandoned, but would suddenly break into surprisingly cheerful red flowers. The flowers hung, pendulous on bulbous stalks, and could be pleasingly popped open between finger and thumb to reveal the even more surprising inner petals of garish purple. There were three hydrangea bushes too, but they were never surprising or cheerful. They had watery blue flowers which shrivelled quickly into sorrowful brown heads that reminded me of drizzly autumn afternoons.

The front garden, however, was my refuge. It was long and narrow too, like a shadow of the gaunt house behind it. There was a crunching gravel driveway and a grassy lawn that was speckled with daisies and some smiling yellow flowers that looked like dandelions, but were actually some other species. There was a granite wall at the front of the garden with ridiculously pompous granite gateposts and a wooden gate that wasn't quite white and was never closed anyway, but always hung squeaking restlessly on its hinges. The garden wall was masked from the house by a clumpy row of seedy bamboo, that fretted in the slightest breeze and would be treated with contempt by any self-respecting panda.

Sitting on the wall, masked by the bamboo from the peevish, tiny eyes of the narrow dark house, I could gaze across the road and down the hill over the rooftops to the sea. I was a lonely, scrawny, frightened child with no friends, and I would often while away long hours watching the sea. Although the sea scared me, for I could see its sudden savagery often enough, its permanent indifference gave me comfort. It neither laughed at me, nor teased me, nor scolded me, but every morning, huge as the sky, it would be there. It was a fixed security amongst all my timid uncertainties, but with all the moods and characters of an ancient god. Indeed, for several years, between the ages of about six and twelve, or probably longer, I would utter up hopeful prayers towards it, tasting the salt and seaweed on my lips and trying to read answers and promises of fulfilment in the grey-blue hazy sparkle or in the dirty white wave crests when the wind was brisk.

Where does childhood begin and where does it end? For me, that is an easy question. I can almost give exact dates. For me, childhood began, in that I became aware of my own, awkward, shabby existence in the world, when Ziggy was seven years old. It began when he left our narrow world of the tall dark house with a view of the sea from the garden wall, to attend a boys' preparatory school somewhere in England – Sussex, Surrey or Suffolk, I forget which. I was four years old.

I remember walking to the station with Ziggy and Aunt Bernice on a cold, raw, blustery day in mid-September. His roped-up trunk had been sent ahead by train the week before, and he was following after it. The station was near the docks, and the chill wind whipped up around our faces a dominant, masculine smell of burning rope and paint and greasy rags. Ziggy was wearing shorts and a schoolboy's cap was awry on his blond curls. I remember how mottled and bruised with cold his thin knees looked and how tightly he was gripping his canvas bag; his knuckles were yellowish-white with the effort.

I remember how he said goodbye to us, seven-year-old Ziggy who had never travelled by train before, had never left Cornwall before and had never been anywhere on his own. He took off his cap with his left hand and then shook hands with both of us, first myself, his four-year-old sister, and then Aunt Bernice. Aunt Bernice seemed unaware of the incongruity and made no effort to kiss him or even hug him. He was as upright, formal and cold as any well-seasoned, well-travelled cynic, and he walked on to the platform past the dozing guard, and did not look back. I could see the wind tearing about him on the empty, grubby platform, the cloth of his thin jacket bunched backwards and pushed hard against his jutting shoulder blades. We did not stay to watch him board the train (Aunt Bernice passed a chink of coins to a stout, red-faced porter to ensure that Ziggy managed to leave in good order), and we toiled back home, under the railway bridge, past the docks entrance and up the hill.

The house seemed colder and darker and taller than ever without Ziggy and I felt frightened by its human emptiness and the shadows lurking amongst the crouching furniture.

What a strange, silent, narrow childhood it was. I went to the local primary school for girls, and found no friendship or laughter there. I was easily teased, but I neither cried nor reported the outrages of children's evil to the teachers, and thus I was fair game. 'Zag-the-Bag' they called me in the high, taunting, shrill voices of children, and I would cower in the forbidden area of the school yard at breaks between lessons, behind the bins, and hope that they would not find me, but they inevitably did. They were children that dwarfed me physically, mentally and emotionally, and I offered not even a whimper of resistance. Hooting and jeering they would descend upon me, fingers stretched out like talons, to prod and pinch and poke, with all the wicked viciousness that children excel at.

There was Kate Robinson, chunky and dark and determinedly pretty, leading the sport with all the assurance and self-confidence of the popular and the clever. Her second-in-command, Samantha Crookshaw, was tall and thin, etiolated as though grown in the dark, but there was all the power needed for a brisk, hard kick in those slender legs in grey schoolgirl socks, and my scrawny calves had matt purple-blue bruises that faded to a sick yellow, to prove it. Then followed the seething, merciless rabble of the rank and file: Olivia Middleton, Jane Parfitt, Morwenna Trerice, Nicola Pollard, Katherine Hicks and so many more. Their names and jeering, mocking faces rise before me, even now, like sinful demons out of some eternal fires of hell.

Children are neither subtle nor imaginative in their torments, and they seldom become wearied by repetition of their favourite forms of torture. They would hustle me from my sad, hopeless position of defence behind the clattering bins in a press-gang throng of children, drunk on power. In the whitewashed toilet block at the furthest end of the dusty, eddying yard they would exercise their skills of torture and subjugate me to pointless, bitter acts of humiliation. They made me lick the urine-speckled wooden seats of the child-sized toilets; I can recall now the feel of the hard cold concrete floor under my knees and the rough rasp of the salt, sour wood against my tongue. They made me take off my knickers and flush them down the cistern, so that for the rest of the day my bottom was bare and vulnerable beneath my skirt. My torturers could then easily be entertained by trying to flick up my skirt to expose to the uncaring, sneering world a brief glimpse of my frightened and ashamed buttocks.

The favourite game, however, was to hold me against the wooden door of the end cubicle and, arms above my head, secure me there by drawing pins, pushed in hard to the door by eager thumbs, through the cuffs and sleeves of my grey school shirt. The icing on this particular trick, for those cruel, laughing eyes, was to pin my wretched, skimpy, matted-blonde plaits into the door too, rising vertically above my head. The bell would ring for the start of lessons, and they would run away shrieking and giggling, hands clasped to their delighted mouths, leaving pinioned a helpless, silent, struggling insect against the door. I would yank my arms free first, and often the pins would leave tiny rips in my shirt as though mice had been experimentally nibbling. Those small jagged holes in my uniform would cause problems with Aunt Bernice at home, but the future is always easier to face than the present, especially for a child, for whom time is a strange and undefined concept, devoid of boundaries. I dreaded to be caught by a teacher in that humiliating position of pathetic, elongated crucifixion against the toilet door. With my hands free, I could tug loose my plaits, and leaving a trail of brass-headed pins behind me hurry

19

shamefaced into the classroom to be met by the sly smirks and giggles of my schoolmates, and frequently a sharp reprimand from the teacher about my scuttling lateness and my tousled appearance.

Those stern, silly teachers must have known, or guessed, that I was the object of such merciless, miserable bullying, but their intervention was worse than negligible. When they did intervene, for example the time that thin-faced Miss Hanshaw could not even pretend not to have seen Katherine Maynard smearing fingers dipped in permanent black ink down my history book, and sent her to stand outside the classroom door, I cringed even more in my tiny, withered soul. Punishment meted out to my oppressors, I paid for hugely in the retribution stakes.

Why did those teachers allow that scapegoat suffering to pass unheeded under their very noses? I suppose that I was just categorized as a failure in everything, and allowed to stay like that. My family background was odd, and possibly embarrassing. My guardian, Aunt Bernice, was unapproachable, silent and rancid. She was also not visibly wealthy. I was not a pretty, physically appealing child, with my smileless mouth and my eyes too big for my meagre, pinched face, my hair straggling and imprisoned in awkward plaits, and my arms, legs and shoulders thin and lost. Nor did I shine in my lessons as a repressed and tortured genius should, or show merit in games or athletics. For those teachers, there was not a solitary spark there (other than my existence as a human child, and this was obviously not enough), that made me into material worth encouraging or protecting.

One particular spring-sunshine, hummocky morning in school, I was gazing out of the window over the slate roof of the church with its blue and gold clock, to the white sails of boats, darting across the sparkling harbour in a frisky breeze. The lesson, history or possibly English, was drifting past me as usual, while I indulged in my regular hobby of escapism – day-dreaming about Ziggy – when a sentence, a phrase, all unbidden came creeping from the lesson into my conscious mind. How any phrase could manage to break through my well-fortified mental defences I do not know, and of the remainder of the lesson, these incongrous, isolated, four words were the only ones I heard. The words were '. . . one of life's unfortunates . . .' With dread, I realized that those sneaking words which had invaded my personal space belonged to me. Worse; they were me. I was eight years old.

I would be wrong to describe my frugal life with Aunt Bernice, of long, long evenings of straight-backed silence, as miserably unhappy. It was not, but it was not a happy existence either. Aunt Bernice's knowledge of child-rearing was derived entirely from her own upbringing, in which her brothers, now both long since dead and no more than tired sepia print photographs aloof on the dressing table in her room, were sent away to school to do splendid things. Meanwhile she and her younger sister, Eveline, stayed at home and learned to be silent unless spoken to, humourless and unflinching as granite, and entirely resigned to their lot, whatever their lot turned out to be. Eveline's lot had turned out to be a loveless marriage to a poisonously tyrannical business man in London, which she bore childlessly with all the stoicism that her childhood had trained her for, until he was messily killed in a train crash. Despite his obviously being a callous, unfaithful husband, his death was a mighty blow to Eveline. To return to the town of her birth, her roots and her family would have been regarded as defeat. She was not defeated, she was resigned, and she remained in London, living alone in her basement flat, a sad, humble existence shared only with her cats. Her fortnightly letter from her sister Bernice was one of her few diversions.

If life had managed to pass by Eveline, it had given Bernice an even wider berth. Bernice had never left the home where she was born, the home of my childhood. She had never had friends and had barely even met people, but she stayed, boxed in her narrow existence with her parents, silent and solitary, crocheting anti-macassars and reading the bible. Even the bible was restricted, only selected pieces were allowed; the Old Testament was, for example, much too, well, pagan. She nursed her parents in their decaying old age and through their sickly, petulant senility, until, almost suddenly, they were dead. Two heart attacks and she was alone.

Aunt Bernice met my mother at the long wooden counter of the draper's shop in town shortly after my parents had moved to that part of Cornwall. My mother was whimsically strange, even then, and absorbed almost fully in her husband; she had no close friends. She was kind too, however, and saw beyond the silent, austere acidity of Aunt Bernice to the anger and sadness of the long-suffocated human core, and she felt sorry for her. Why and how and of what they first started talking, I know not, but nevertheless, my pitiful, pitiable mother became Aunt Bernice's first, and possibly only, real friend. Pity seldom changes anything, and the sad, grey, humourless existence that Aunt Bernice was leading me along, was moulding me into a drab caricature of her own unhappy self. If other events had not taken over, I would probably still be living in that haunted, hunted, narrow house with a view of the careless sea from the garden wall, treating humour with suspicion and laughter with the despairing hate that is born of envy.

How did time pass in that strange, long-ago life of childhood when I wasn't at school, day-dreaming and sidestepping learning, and being humiliated and tormented by my contemporaries? When it wasn't raining, I would try to flee from myself by crouching on the garden wall behind the tussle of bamboos, facing the sea, kicking and scuffing my shoes on the hard, winking granite, dreaming unlikely dreams of Ziggy and praying to the glimmering distance of the waves. Inside the house there was a never-ending cycle of petty jobs awaiting me. Old silver cutlery to be polished with elbow grease and last week's newspaper, potatoes to be finely peeled, recalcitrant buttons to be sewn on to formless grey clothes, and aged pillow cases to be darned. I cannot remember ever being told by Aunt Bernice to do these tedious tasks, but they would be there waiting for me accusingly at my corner of the scrubbed wood kitchen table. I knew that they had to be done, and I knew that there would be no shirking or mutters of complaint. Then I did my homework, badly, blotchily, dreamily; muddling amphibians with reptiles, adjectives with adverbs, percentages with fractions, all in the cold, wordless silence of impoverished communication.

What did Aunt Bernice do all this time, and during the hours when I was safely despatched to school? She slaved in a pointless, endless martyrdom to the gods of household work, scrubbing the lino on the kitchen floor, washing by hand in biting cold water the clothes and bed linen and blankets, trudging morosely through the town to find the cheapest, meanest food and then boiling it into a miserable pottage of ambiguity. Of course, if all other inspiration failed her, there was always the relentless crocheting of antimacassars.

On Saturdays in winter it always seemed to be half-past six in the evening. Too late to be in the garden, too early to be in bed. The daily household chores completed, we would sit in the kitchen at the wooden table, scrubbed that day with cold, soapsuddy water, in silence. Aunt Bernice would be crocheting an antimacassar (as well as draped on the backs of the lumbering old chairs, she had piles of these ridiculous objects crammed into fusty drawers), and I would

23

simply do nothing. It was not until secondary school that I discovered books, and up until the age of eleven, my Saturday nights were composed of a straight-backed waiting for the clock finally to tick its way to eight. At eight I could slide from my hard wooden chair, kiss Aunt Bernice on her sour, sallow cheek and scuttle through the amorphous shadows of lonely fear to my chilly bed. I was a fine student in the school of grim resignation.

On Sundays there was church in both the mornings and the evenings, a Sunday lunch of a poor roasted something, usually either beef or chicken, cooked to a dry, ungiving solidity, and stiff, slow readings of the bible. The bible was a big, black, heavy, leatherbound affair. A family bible that went back through the generations of Aunt Bernice's family, it was an object of fear and awe to both of us.

How we prayed and prostrated ourselves on Sundays, Aunt Bernice and I, my chill, thin form bending and bobbing in the gloom of her appointed shadow. I prayed for the soul of the father I never knew and his gloves that I knew intimately, I prayed for my poor, derelict mother, but mostly I prayed for Ziggy. I don't know what Aunt Bernice prayed for, but I would guess that it wasn't so very different – her own brothers had been demigods to her, with wonderful, unimaginable powers. There was obviously something very special about being a boy. I say that I prayed for Ziggy, but really I prayed to him. I venerated his unknown fraternal presence, as Aunt Bernice had so clearly worshipped her own brothers.

Then, every other Sunday after tea, always something stodgily plain and purportedly wholesome, Aunt Bernice would sit at the kitchen table and slowly, laboriously compose her letter to her widowed sister in London, Eveline. News was always scant and Aunt Bernice's prose dry and fustily monotonous. The letter was merely one of the rituals that spelled out her existence, otherwise she would surely never have bothered.

Holiday time I always saw in glorious colours. Ziggy would arrive by train, always a little older, always a little taller, always a little more resentful of his worshipping younger sister, always a little more sour and unsmiling at slotting into the silent tedium of home existence with Aunt Bernice, always looking for ways to escape.

Each holiday we would make one dreary trip to Bodwell to visit our mother. We would have to be up early and have a bath. Ziggy had the first bath, and I would use the tepid scummy water that he left in the tub. It would be grey, slimy water and the soap would be etched with blond curls of hair; it seemed the natural order to me. We would have to wear our best clothes and be on our best behaviour, but I was a drooping, meek, resigned little creature that only had best behaviour anyway.

Mother would always look older than the last time. Her face bagged and sagged into coarse, bewildered folds, and she dribbled and squawked like a wild waterfowl. Sometimes she would recognize us, but most frequently she did not. She smelt of staleness and urine and old, hardening sweat. It was no more pleasure to kiss her than to kiss Aunt Bernice, and for a long time I associated kissing with the long, sour smell of age and decay.

We three would sit around her in hopeless, taciturn awkwardness, while the efficient nurses would briskly chat to us, bayoneting our useless reticence with sensible questions. Aunt Bernice would remain pinioned in her expression of wrinkled, tough, mean austerity and Ziggy's face would be a mask of irritation. If Mother was particularly wild or unpredictable he would flash accusing glances of resentment at me, for he knew where the blame lay. I would be trapped too, in an expression of resignation, boredom, timidity and guilt. Even now, it is the natural cast of my features in repose.

At eleven years of age, I left primary school and started at secondary school. I was still very much a child, but things had changed. The first major change had been initiated three years previously, when Ziggy had progressed from his preparatory school to the glorious, heady heights of a distant public school. To begin with this had had no impact on my life, but suddenly it did. I realized that Ziggy had friends. It was a punching, winding shock to me that left me scared and bewildered. What was all the more confusing was that Aunt Bernice encouraged these friends; at least she made a valiant attempt to do so – encouragement was not her particular forte. I had not been allowed the luxury of friendship at all, the very idea had been repressed and crushed, leaving only despair and loneliness. With Ziggy it was different. I felt bitterly jealous and abandoned. Why was it so different being a boy?

The Christmas that followed my eleventh birthday hit me with a callous blow. Ziggy did not come home for the holiday – he had gone to stay with a friend. Christmas, never a festive occasion anyway in our grim household, became even less joyous. Yet, despite my devouring jealousy, anger and throbbing hurt, the desperate prayers I offered up on my thin knees from the cold slate floor of the parish church on Christmas Day were, more than ever before, both for and to Ziggy. He was a mighty and exalted being to whom I was in debt from birth, and now he had friends.

The second major change in my restricted life was the clean sweep of school contemporaries. A chance for my own fresh start. No more Kate Robinson, Samantha Crookshaw and all their fearsome ranks of friends and allies, for they had gone to the local secondary school, whereas I made the glorious hour-long bus journey every day to the girls' grammar school in Trelvo. Clearly it was not academic achievement that sent me there, but the hard, cold clink of the only currency that ever really counts in this world. I knew not how, I did not question why, I merely accepted it with a grateful relief and took the bus to and from Trelvo every day.

Sadly, of course, my hopes of a fresh start were not to be entirely fulfilled. My scapegoat image clung to me like a foul aroma, and again I became the butt of cruel jokes and malicious humour. Yet it was never so bad as those primary-school days, and the usual cheers of 'Here comes the Bodwell Bastard,' and 'Zag-the-Rag is a slag,' and the jeering taunts of 'Where's yer loony mum?' were frail pebbles hurled at my resigned, unflinching face compared with the previously-flung boulders. I was still lost in hopeful, hopeless dreams during my lessons and I still failed to learn. I was still a pinched, ugly creature, unsure of everything and feebly poor at sports, but I felt safe, and I also came across, through school, my third major influence of the time.

The school, which was relatively wealthy, had a library and I discovered the joyous escapism of books. At first Aunt Bernice was suspicious and fretful of my time-devouring hobby, but she was convinced by the school crest stamped on the front page of every book that they must be worthy objects of my attention, and although she sniffed and glinted her eyes menacingly, she never prevented me from reading or censored my taste. The Saturday evenings of the resigned tedium of waiting were never long enough now, as I galloped from page to printed page, hungering for more and more. I read greedily and uncritically, feasting on stories and imagination of which I had been previously starved.

It was, as I said, escapism. Of course it was, but it was a wild, savage, solitary and yet permissible escapism. I was hooked as quickly and fiercely as any addict, and that addiction led, as it inevitably does, to deception. It was my first, tentative step away from the Aunt Bernice School of Resignation. I entered into my first liaison with deceit and theft. I stole time and misled trust, smuggling a torch into my cold, dark, dingy, high-ceilinged cell of a bedroom, that I might, under the coarse hairiness of the blankets in my narrow bed, continue reading. I felt a wicked thrill at the success of my secret plots and well-hidden triumphs. The skinny hands of Aunt Bernice that had clutched me in, to be her replica of sullen, silent, sour submission, had no hold where books were concerned. It was the first notion of another life and the first whiff of a struggle to escape.

Chapter Four

There was one summer that lay upon Cornwall in a splintering heat. The sky seemed to have melted and then evaporated into a smouldering haze. The grass on the front lawn crackled menacingly underfoot, and the whole world seemed fissile and ready to explode. The sea was the merest breath of cool sweetness drifting across the town, and Aunt Bernice, surprisingly, allowed me to go to the beach every evening after school to swim. I suppose it would have been physically cruel to have forbidden me, and, for all her harsh, sour misery, Aunt Bernice was not a cruel woman. I never went with a friend to swim off the gritty gold sand beach, for I didn't have one, but I always took a book to read. I was an uncritical, logical reader. After my swim, I would sprawl on the beach and devour a book with a hungry greed, and then, unsatiated, move swiftly on to whatever novel or treatise I had picked up next. I was twelve years old.

Although Ziggy had ceased to come home to Cornwall for both the Christmas and Easter holidays, always able to take up an invitation with those unknown aliens called friends, he returned to us every summer. I knew it was because he loved to be by the sea, but I often hoped it was, perhaps only slightly, because he wanted to see me. This particular blazing, dazzling summer, the unexpected came to us. To the strange, silent, narrow house of my strange, silent, narrow childhood, Ziggy brought a friend.

We both went to the station to meet them off the train, Aunt Bernice and I, and the usual silence between us on the dusty platform seemed to me to be loud with anxiety. I felt a sagging pit of nervousness in my stomach, that perhaps seems out of proportion now. It was the fear of rejection. I knew that we were both odd, peculiar, unlikeable characters, for my schooldays taught me that, if nothing else, but I wanted to be accepted now, more than I had ever wanted anything before.

Despite this stomach-hollow fear, despite the short letter in schoolboy-bold script that Ziggy had written to Aunt Bernice to tell her that Dobson (that was his name, Arthur Dobson) was coming home with him (Aunt Bernice had tutted her pursed lips with a furious irritation, and then shrugged her shoulders with her usual, shrew-sharp, resigned twitch), I was still surprised to see the two boys jumping down from the dirt-streaked train into a pool of sunlit dust. It had seemed so improbable. First came wonderful Ziggy, fifteen years old, awkward, gangly, even pimply with adolescence, but still the object of my complete adoration, and then close behind him, Dobson.

Even before I had consciously registered him I had committed Dobson to my memory. Other than myself, Ziggy, Aunt Bernice and the coalmen, he was the first person that I knew to enter that dark home of ours. He was, all unknowingly, an explorer in a strange uncharted land. He was not a good-looking boy, short, stocky and peculiarly hirsute. Black coarse hair roamed over his neck and arms (the boys were both in short-sleeved school shirts), and sprouted in unkempt tufts from between his thick eyebrows and from around his ears. There was a faint, scrubby shadowiness about his mouth and chin where a moustache and beard were pushing to thrust their way through, and he had an overhanging curvature of the spine, which humped his back and shoulders slightly but perceptibly. He was swarthily dark-skinned too, as though some Mediterranean ancestry

30

was lurking beneath his very English name (at the time I thought he must be partially Turkish) and his eyes were beadily brown and bloodshot. He was totally unlike what I had imagined, although I don't suppose I had really imagined anybody, but he was Ziggy's friend, and I loved him on the spot, for being just that.

I believe that Aunt Bernice really tried to like Dobson, tried to be polite and unwind from her sour, crackling crabbiness, tried to act correctly, to be hospitable and to do the right thing, but even with the best will in the world she could not succeed. It was an experience that she was encountering too late in life to unbend her, and after an initial exhausting effort she relapsed into her normal pattern. She was, perhaps, even more awkward, angular, morose and taciturn than usual, and I felt impelled to try to take over as the courteous, charming hostess. I was ill-prepared for such a role, and, worse still, Ziggy didn't want me to try. Again and again the feelings of being spurned, rejected and unwanted brought hot, hurt tears to my eyes, as the boys bolted their breakfasts and ricocheted out of the house to the beach.

Sometimes I managed to go with them and tried to ingratiate myself into their uninterested company. I tried to ignore their unsubtle signs that shrieked out to the whole world that they did not want to know me. Their conversations were of an excluding secrecy, and even when Ziggy didn't actually tell me in so many words to leave them alone, but let me stay and listen, drinking in their words with an eagerness that must have been flattering, I did not, could not, understand them. They spoke in a strange language, a semi-English that revolved around, and was derived from, their school. Their sentences were studded with fantastic, unknown words like 'baggers' and 'clouties' and 'feltoes', and I felt my feeble, female ignorance swamping me in huge waves of envy. I would leave them

31

sprawled on the sand and, perched on a distant rock with the sea trickling between my toes, would divide my time between worshipping from a distance and avidly reading. Ziggy and Dobson were even more important than my books, but, heedless boys, they trampled my hopes into the gritty sand. Nevertheless, it was my best summer ever, and the nagging pain of loss that I felt with their departure in September is still memorable.

We saw them off at the station in the afternoon, and the lengthening shadows cloaked the station forecourt in a chilly gloom that belied the dancing blue of the sky. Dobson thanked Aunt Bernice politely, with all the manners of refinement his upbringing and school had entrenched in him. He gave me a gentle punch on my shoulder and told me what a 'sport' I'd been. Although I knew I hadn't been a sport at all, although I knew how much I'd simply been a useful slave and an unwanted clinging limpet, I flushed with pleasure. Not surprising really, it was the first compliment, true or false, that I had ever received.

The house seemed horribly quiet and empty when we got home. Aunt Bernice set to work to strip the boys' beds, tutting and frowning with irritation. I left her to it, and went and sat on the sun-warmed garden wall and offered up my prayers to the bright, bright blue laughter of the summer sea. I prayed for my father, I prayed for my mother, I prayed for Ziggy and I prayed for Dobson.

The following winter was shiveringly cold, as though a punishment for the frivolous heat of the summer. Not as cold as the winter of my birth, but bitter nevertheless, with brief flurried scatterings of snow (unusual in Cornwall) and the puddles glazed to crackling ice. Ziggy went to stay with Dobson's family in Gloucestershire for Christmas, and Dobson sent me a Christmas card. It was a perfectly boring, plain, cheap, ordinary Christmas card, with the unexciting words

'To Zag, Happy Christmas, from A. Dobson'

printed inside. I blushed with pleasure and shame as I read it. Aunt Bernice sniffed disapprovingly when she saw it; I liked to think that she was jealous. I kept it for a long time, using it as a bookmark.

Just three days before Christmas, Aunt Bernice received a telegram. It was in a plain yellow envelope and smelt of pepper and trouble. Aunt Bernice's widowed sister, Eveline, had died; it was probably hypothermia. There was, it seemed, no heating at all in that lonesome basement flat of hers in London. Much later I found out that she must have been dead for over a fortnight when she was finally discovered, curled into a blanket on a chair. The cold had meant that she had not decayed at all, but her cats were hungry and half her face had been gnawed away. And so, the day after Boxing Day, we went to London.

I had never been outside Cornwall before, but, as trained to do so, viewed the trip with resignation rather than excitement. I took a sizeable stack of books to read on the train, and Dobson's Christmas card tucked inside each one as it was greedily devoured, marked my passage through them. I also took those brown wool gloves of my father, packed neatly into their tobacco tin. I don't know why I took them; I suppose they were the only possessions I had any feelings of affection for.

Aunt Bernice took a large hunk of yarn and a crochet hook, but sitting opposite her on the train, I could observe that the speed of antimacassar production had slowed. She seemed very tightly buttoned up some-how, squashed into herself almost. As we crossed the Tamar out of Cornwall, the mists rising from the river and drifting through the black bulges of Brunel's bridge, I looked eagerly across at Aunt Bernice and I was struck by the military stiffness of her shoulders.

I recognized the upright rigidity as apprehension, even dread. She too had never left Cornwall before and feared the strange lands beyond. I realize now that she was also facing with fear the known yet unknown spectre of death. Eveline, her younger sister, unseen for so many uncounted years, had set out on both these unknown adventures in advance of Aunt Bernice. Perhaps she was even a trifle jealous.

London is an overcrowded place to be at any time, but around Christmas and New Year its hectic bustle is particularly marked. This was true at that time too, almost thirty years ago. Consequently, it was not easy to find somewhere to stay. Aunt Bernice seemed to feel that a hotel was the correct and proper place to stay, but the only hotel rooms that were free were to be found in the grand and palatial suites, and that would never do. It wasn't so much the cost that was restrictive, but the idea that we would be residing in unaccustomed luxurious splendour that would not suit our circumstances at all. The only reason we were in London was to tidy away those sad remains of Eveline, and for that purpose our living accommodation required a certain austerity, a certain measure of Spartan gloominess that might be more appropriate for the contemplation of death and the disintegration of existence. After perhaps an hour of anxious enquiry under the splendid high glass roof of Paddington station, Aunt Bernice decided that we should take some rooms in a respectable house in Stoney Street, in the dull shadows of Southwark Cathedral.

To take rooms in London nowadays is not so easily done. The idea was little more than an ancestor to Bed and Breakfast, and even then it was an antiquated notion; perhaps that is why it appealed to Aunt Bernice. There is a solid feeling of resigned perma-nence embodied in the very expression 'taking rooms', and although we had no intentions of staying any longer than a week, there was a vaguely comforting feeling of belonging.

Stoney Street was a handy location for our purpose. Eveline's basement flat was not so far away in Lamond Street in Bermondsey, and the lawyers, Messrs Thwaite, Thwaite and Higgens, in whose capable legal hands Eveline's meagre affairs were residing, not far either, across the Thames in Fenchurch Street.

We had a bedroom each in our set of rooms on the second floor of the house in Stoney Street, each with a squidgy-mattressed bed, orange flock wallpaper and each carpeted in a pattern of bright red with yellow, semi-heraldic symbols. It was an affront to the eye really, but seemed alive and cheery to me, so used to the dingy, dark furnishings of home. There was a narrow black and white tiled bathroom of curious wedge-shaped proportions with a high white iron bath standing on curling lion's paws between our bed-rooms. We ate downstairs on the ground floor in a large draughty dining room, with the other half-dozen people who had taken rooms in the house. All this was presided over by our landlady, a stout, red-faced, sausage-fingered widow, once married to an Irish labourer. Her name was Mrs O'Cavanagh.

Aunt Bernice decided immediately that it would not be the proper thing for me to accompany her on her ventures between the paper-faced lawyers and Eveline's empty flat. It was not to be done. However, on our first full day in London, 28 December, it was Eveline's funeral; this event I had to attend.

It was a grim, chill, blustery day as is befitting of funerals, and Aunt Bernice and I, bundled into our respectful clothes of a faded, weeping black, took a taxi to the cemetery in East Dulwich to be sole mourners at Eveline's interment in the grave next to that of her husband. It was the first funeral I'd ever been to (my father had been buried in Kenya), and the shabby, pompous solemnity of the occasion caught at my stifled imagination. The lonely ridiculousness of the event snatched at my lost emotions, and the thin drizzle of tears on my wind-nipped cheeks was very real. I was not crying for the unknown Eveline, of course, but for myself. A funeral without love or affection or loss is a miserable thing indeed, and the horror struck deep into my lonely, emaciated soul that both Aunt Bernice and I were likely to have similarly drear and loveless endings.

On the way to the cemetery Aunt Bernice had stopped the taxi twice as we passed rows of grey, deadpan shops. She was attempting to buy some flowers. The chill frosts and the festive time of year, however, left the shops bereft of any types of plants apart from mistletoe and holly. At the second stop Aunt Bernice bought a small sprig of holly, which, at the East Dulwich cemetery, she placed on the plain wood coffin. If anything that incongruous, cheery touch of red and green, glistening in the drab grey of the cold graveyard, accentuated the pathos.

'Like a bleedin' Christmas pud,' I heard one of the broad, foot-stamping coffin-bearers mutter hoarsely to another, but it could have been worse; it could have been a lonely, decaying vigil under a sprig of mistletoe, waiting for ever to be kissed.

How Aunt Bernice felt as we watched the coffin being lowered, slowly, bumpily, into the frost-hardened, rimey ground, no less friendly and possibly no less warm than Eveline's basement flat, it was impossible to make out. She had withdrawn into her sour, shrunken self and any feeling seemed to be either drained or smothered. A few soulless words were said by some unknown religious figure with a cockney cold and a long quivering nose, and then we took the taxi back to Stoney Street. The journey was wordless as ever, but Aunt Bernice gave the driver a generously clinking tip and slammed the door with a gusto that hinted at some sort of emotion; something that was only very rarely discernible in her.

The next five or six days were strange ones for me, and remarkable ones also. Aunt Bernice would leave Stoney Street as soon as our breakfast of hot buttered toast and marmalade and hot strong tea was finished. She seemed to be extremely busy, seeing the lawyers, house-clearers, dealers, property owners and that amorphous group of shabby individuals that, thankfully, seem to exist no more, who bought up pets who have outlived their owners for experimental purposes in laboratories, questing for answers to our ills. She would return to Stoney Street when it was long gone five and the evening was already dark, and although she took care not to appear flustered, her crabbiness and sourness were diminished by a weary anxiety. In short, I had the whole day alone, and nowhere to go; London was cold and its unknown, hustling, rushing busyness terrified me.

In no time at all our Stoney Street landlady, Mrs O'Cavanagh, had taken me under her wing, and what a wing it was. It was a noisy, laughing, chattering, joking, never-endingly amused and warming wing. It was a generous, comforting wing that hinted to me of the power of humour and the glow brought by friendly, bodily contact. It was a wing that provided immense instruction to my sour innocence, and it was instruction that I delighted to bask and wallow in. I suppose that Mrs O'Cavanagh was a lonely lady, and to have me creeping willingly, ready to listen, into the warmth of her cosy kitchen where she prepared the meals for myself, Aunt Bernice and the six other residents, brought pleasure to her too. I sincerely hope so, for it would be nice to feel that I had paid, in some small measure, for the gifts she showered upon me; the realization that human warmth and generosity of spirit existed, and the initiation into a lasting preference for sitting in an active kitchen rather than any other room in a house.

Aunt Bernice left the house in Stoney Street in the morning with brief, clipped instructions to me,

'Be good and mind you don't get under Mrs O'Cavanagh's feet.'

No sooner had the front door clunked shut than Mrs O'Cavanagh would whisk me from out of the hallway into the cosy, steaming bustle of her kitchen.

'It's the only room in the house you'll be warm in,' she would cluck. 'We can't have a poor little mite like you freezing to death under our very noses, can we?' Then perhaps feeling that she'd made a terrible faux pas (for she knew how Eveline, so recently buried, had died) she would straight away, although breakfast had only just been cleared, be pouring me fat, chipped mugs of a tea so sweet and strong that it kicked. While she buried her fat, rolling arms into the steamy suds of the washing-up she would encourage me to nibble into her glistening, uneven circles of homemade spiced ginger biscuits. In Aunt Bernice's household, tea and biscuits was considered a ridiculous frivolity, almost verging on the sinful, that would be sure to wreak terrible damage on your appetite; inevitably I loved tea and biscuits, particularly straight after breakfast. However, it wasn't so much this frivolous munching in which I really luxuriated in this happy kitchen, but the ceaseless flow of chattering conversation, all of it provided for my delectation alone. Mrs O'Cavanagh had so many fascinating topics that she could talk on endlessly, the words rolling and tumbling from her lips in rich delicious handfuls like globules of honey or golden syrup. Inevitably, I suppose, her favourite topic was the lodgers.

'There's Mr and Mrs Washington, of course. You're sure to have noticed them in the dining room. They get the best seats, next to the window. They pay for that, as an extra, you understand. Not that it's much of a view at all. In fact, I don't know why they bother. Very tall is Mr Washington, have you noticed? Oh, very tall he is, and quite a gentleman I should say. There must be money somewhere in there, you only have to look at their clothes to tell that. I really don't know why they're staying with me anyway. They don't say and I don't ask. That's a good motto I think, don't you? If you ask you're bound to lose your illusions somehow. Mind you, if that wife of his, Mrs Washington I'm talking about now, quite a prim little madam she is really, if she says her tea is too stewed once more, I may feel liable to take them to task, I really might. Now, Mr Huddle there, I could never take him to task ever. He's that tiny thin one with the huge drooping moustache. Practically buried under that moustache he is, gets it in his tea the whole time. Must be a nuisance, not that I'd ever say so to him of course. So quiet he is though, and so good. Like a little mouse. Still, my old mum said you should watch the quiet ones. What do you think? She said they're the ones who turn out to be nasty mass murderers and the like. Not Mr Huddle though. No, I don't think so. Too small and frail to murder even a child, and some kids could do with a murdering. Only joking, don't look so shocked. No, he's much too nice. Not like some I could mention . . .'

On and on rolled this endless, streaming torrent of comment, gossip and description, and I would fall helplessly and happily beneath its barrage. I was bewitched by such gems as her descriptions of Mr Stirrup's pyjamas ('pale pink roses; very odd for a gent'), the fate that befell poor, pretty Maisie Joiner ('no, she's no longer staying here, no, no'), and hence why single young women were no longer welcomed into Mrs O'Cavanagh's cheery portals, and the lengths to which tubby Mr Hunnybun ('such a charming young man, too') had to go to secure regular employment in this bad, busy, hectic city. During this verbal bombardment Mrs O'Cavanagh would skip her fat, dancing figure nimbly round the kitchen, preparing the next meals and pouring endless cups of tea for both of us, until, when she came to a particularly engrossing section of her discourse she would stop, and sit down. Then, suddenly it would be nearly lunch time or some such other hour, and she would bounce to her feet (her favourite place to rest her ample weight was a tall wooden three-legged stool) with a vigorous, bustling energy.

'There, there, dearie me. See how you've kept me gossiping again. I don't know. Not that I can blame you, of course. I love a good chat, don't you? Tomorrow I'll be having you telling me all the tales about your home down in the south-west, and about your nice auntie too. Looks a bit down at the moment, she does. Still, to be expected really. Now, how about if you give me a hand and just chop these carrots for me, and we'll be ready in the twinkling of an eye. That's splendid, I don't know how I've managed without you, I really don't. Here, let me give you a big hug and a peck of a kiss on that beautiful wan little cheek of yours. Off you go now, scurry into the dining room and sit yourself down and I'll bring it all through to you in half a mo'. It's a delicious steamed jam pudding too today, you'll like that. Off you flit now, and remember to come back in here this afternoon if you've got nothing better to do.'

All this in a busy welter of steamy activity, a few suffocatingly close hugs of genuine affection, in which I sank into Mrs O'Cavanagh's mountainous bosom as though into a soft and friendly quagmire, and some loud rich smacking kisses on both my cheeks. I was totally absorbed in the happy conviviality of Mrs O'Cavanagh and her warm, bubbling kitchen, and to emerge into the cold white light of Aunt Bernice was like being slapped across the face by an icy and long-dead herring. Not a pleasant awakening to that other world in which I really existed.

*   *   *

40

How I relished and glorified in the churning flow of Mrs O'Cavanagh's conversation. How I loved to hear tales of her married life to Joe, the Irish labourer, killed three years ago in a manner that I found, somehow, appropriate. Drunk, as any good Irishman should be on St Patrick's day, he had staggered into, and then tumbled under, a number 27 bus at Cambridge Circus, although a 27 bus, so Mrs O'Cavanagh said, should never have been there anyway. Tears trickled down her red face as she described, in Technicolor detail, Joe's death. Even her tears, round sparkles of imitation diamonds, seemed to be peculiarly joyful and full of a zest for life. She cried openly, unashamed to let her feelings be seen, although she rubbed away the evidence briskly on a large white handkerchief. There was a red J embroidered on the corner of the handkerchief, Joe's handkerchief, and when she saw it Mrs O'Cavanagh was awash again with further tears. She gathered me up in her great, fat, wonderful arms, my face squashed between the pillows of her breasts, and she blubbed loudly and wetly into my hair. Not for long however, for the passage of time could not be halted for tearful outbursts, and before long she was bustling busily and merrily around the kitchen again.

'Nearly time for dinner, Zag dear. What a truly funny name that is. I know I'll never get used to it. Still, your poor tired auntie will be home soon, so will you just give me a quick hand, dear? Slice up that onion perhaps. All this crying and talk of death can't be good for us. Good to have it aired though, don't you think? If Joe's watching, and I'm sure he is, he'll be pleased to see I haven't forgotten him. Look at the lovely pud I've made for you tonight. What's your auntie's favourite pud? You don't know? Shame on you! I was hoping to make her favourite tomorrow, because I have just the slightest sneaking suspicion that she isn't eating properly. The worry, you know. All bone she is, and skin

41

too I suppose, but no fat at all. You need a bit of padding on you in this cruel weather. Thank you dearie. That's the door now, so you just come and give me a quick hug and scoot off into the dining room to see your auntie. No more talk of death and funerals tomorrow, OK?'

Tomorrow came, and the next day too, and even I started, under Mrs O'Cavanagh's prodding and probing, questioning and suggesting, to talk freely. I talked about Ziggy, my brother, my hero, and I talked about the beautiful, moody sea, and I talked about books. I talked about all the things in my life that spoke to me of happiness and brightness. All the dark, sour bitterness of my family, my friends (or lack of them) and the dank squalor of my inmost soul, I kept shut away and unspoken. I was afraid that if I mentioned these evil miseries, then all the friendly humanity of that warm, steamy, busy kitchen might be submerged and destroyed for ever under the grim malevolence of those dark spirits.

We left Mrs O'Cavanagh's residence in Stoney Street after a week. A taxi picked us up from the front door early in the morning, just as breakfast was being eaten. Mr and Mrs Washington watched us from their seats in the dining-room window, and Mr Washington raised his long, white elegant hand in a silent gesture of goodbye. There were no silent gestures from Mrs O'Cavanagh however, enfolding first Aunt Bernice and then myself in mammoth engulfing farewell hugs. Aunt Bernice extracted herself primly and stiffly, and gave a disapproving sniff that was audible to me even through the untold layers of Mrs O'Cavanagh's bosom. There was a smattering of tears from both our landlady and myself which Aunt Bernice observed with disgust. It is always difficult to say goodbye to an ephemeral bliss. It is to my shame that as Mrs O'Cavanagh slammed shut the taxi door behind us I did not raise a word of protest to Aunt Bernice's comment on the whole transaction. A curt and acid comment.

'I never realized how cheap and nasty that woman was.'

Chapter Five

Jack Lewis came to Cornwall with Ziggy in the summer that year. I began to feel almost worldly or cosmopolitan. Not only had there been the peculiarly welcome week of winter in London, idling away the hours in casual chatter with the widow of an Irish labourer, but now there was a Welshman, silly, soft, singing voice, pudgy, white, hairless knees and all, staying under the same roof as us. Perhaps life and the vast breadth of the world was not entirely swerving past me after all. At least, that is what I hoped, desperate hope against pointless, desperate hope, as I watched the mocking, distant sea from my perch on the garden wall. Yet I knew it was only a pitiful, paper-thin, or even finer, vapour-thin, layer of hope. Every novel that I read with hungry avarice taunted me with the knowledge that my existence was narrow and dull, and the restriction in my life was cruelly mimicked by the constriction of frustrated tears that kept me choked. Mrs O'Cavanagh, in her kind and merry friendliness, had provided me with a glimpse of a change in fortunes. Once back in Cornwall, under the steely chill of the forbidding eyes of my home and my guardian, I crumpled and returned to my former existence of silent bitterness.

The summer arrival of Ziggy and his friend, Jack Lewis, raised my enthusiasm, but as with Dobson's year-past visit, I was immediately relegated to the role of tiresome little sister. This was not so woundingly mortifying as it had felt the previous summer, for I despised Lewis greatly. To define what it was in Lewis,

44

or in myself, that made me feel so unremittingly peeved and so hugely irritated by his very presence is not so simple. Certainly his lilting Welsh valley accent grated, as did his words, trite, foolish platitudes flitting through the murk and shadows of our home, but it was more than that. His obvious devotion to Ziggy I found nauseous (although I was aware of how very hypocritical were my feelings about his attitude towards my glorious golden brother), but it was more than that too. Nor was it merely his soft white physique, like a pallid grub, trapped in immaturity by an inability to metamorphose, although that also repelled me, especially his aforementioned sagging folds of knees. His inability to swim I found pitiful and disgusting, but as a nondescript character at most sport myself, the amount of scorn and loathing incited in me by Lewis's ungainly flailing in the rippling shallows was disproportionate. In retrospect, I suppose it was just another way of expressing the gripping, grasping scour of jealousy and incomprehension. What had this gelatinous dollop of foolish Welshman got, with his clear lack of either mental or physical prowess, that he could command the interest and attentions of Ziggy in a way that I had never managed?

It was not the dazzling, fiery summer of the year before, where almost every breath of scorched daytime air was breathed on the beach, but a more typical, mixed, soft, pearl-grey, Cornish summer, with days of gentle sunshine interspersed with bouts of drizzled mist. The foghorn on the lighthouse across the bay frequently boomed out its echoing, mournful message, and the two boys did not often go to the beach.

Instead they spent much of their time slouching through the town and fishing from the old harbour walls for small, green-slimed, leggy shore-crabs. Those poor unfortunate crabs! Lewis would wrench off their pincers with his brutal, pale, pudgy hands and then Ziggy would toss the mutilated, frantic carcass back

45

into the oily murk of the harbour water, to meet who knows what fate. I never accompanied Lewis and Ziggy on these moody, crab-torturing expeditions. Not only was I uninvited and unwelcome, but I hated to wander through the grey town in case I should have the misfortune to meet any tormentors of my own history. Few demons of my primary-school days would have left the area, and the thought of a chance encounter with Kate Robinson, Samantha Crookshaw or the rest of their vicious disciples twitched alive the chill ribbon of fear still coiled inside me.

Nevertheless, I knew what Ziggy and Lewis were doing on the harbour wall, delving into the dark waters with their fishing lines baited with twists of winkle meat. I knew how they maimed the crabs with their deftly violent hands, for they brought back the crab claws as trophies of their frivolous cruelty. They would leave the claws in a grim victory row on the garden wall, arranged in ascending order of size, with the largest nearest to the creaking, unshut gate. The knowledge of their mindless, mean and petty violence did not affront or shock me. Nor can I remember feelings of dismay or pity. I was a sad, lonesome character but I was not awash with goodness or piety. However, I did feel an impotent empathy for those poor dismembered crabs, and I would bury the pincers in a shallow common grave, an unmarked indentation in the sandy soil between the granite garden wall and the tall whispers of bamboo.

Eventually, of course, Lewis got nipped. Although the crabs are but straggles of crustaceans and not large, they can deal a painful pinch with their claws. Lewis's soft, creamy thumb was marked with a pleasing, cloudy, angry redness that rollicked to a thudding purple bruise. I hoped that the crab had meted out its judgemental nip with its strong and agile pincers and then escaped back into the harbour's silky depths; such an outcome would have provided a chance of elevation for my own maimed emotions. I asked, of course, when Aunt Bernice was out of earshot. Heartless, lilting words from the Welsh valleys,

'I stamped on the bastard, and when that didn't kill him, we burnt his legs off with matches. One by one.'

There was no hope for the tormented helpless after all.

Although when the summer holidays drew to a damp, salty, tepid, cloudy close I was sorry, as always, to see Ziggy leave, it was tinged with the relief that he took with him Lewis. The last I saw of Lewis for many years was the straining grey cloth of his trousers that encased his fat Welsh bottom, flobbling down the sunless station platform behind Ziggy.

The resilience to hard, harsh situations that the human race possesses is an amazing thing, and has been demonstrated and exclaimed over many times. My situation could neither be described as hard nor harsh, but it was a blank, bland, horizonless sea, starkly empty of emotion, and I floundered in it pitifully. Nevertheless, time seemed to pass with extraordinary rapidity after Lewis and Ziggy had left. Christmas swept dutifully past with neither deaths nor trips to London, and I was soon surprised to be waking up to the mown-grass scent of summer that penetrated even our discouraging home. The sky faded into the soft, salty, beckoning blue that meant that the holidays were close, and that also heralded the arrival of Ziggy. This was to be a summer holiday of particular importance for both Ziggy and me, for neither of us would be returning to our schools. Ziggy was nineteen, and I was sixteen years old.

My last day at school was racked with the uncertainty of divided feelings. School had been neither enjoyable nor pleasant; I was academically and intellectually stunted, and nobody seemed to visualize any hopes of improvement. Also, I had failed to obtain the

47

gratification of friendship or even companionship in all those years of school attendance. Nevertheless, school was a routine to which I was accustomed and which I understood. It was, in its own way, a familiar haven. Life, without school, stretched before me as an eternity to be shared with Aunt Bernice. Despite my appointed nature of silent, sour resignation this vision of the future was a grim, unwelcoming prospect from which every narrow cell in my pinched body quailed.

Ziggy probably felt less despondent about his future, but perhaps he was as equally uncertain and anxious. He had no intention of returning to Cornwall, myself, Aunt Bernice and the sundry other yokes of gloom (including our mother, still efficiently incarcerated at Bodwell), and although he had not displayed himself to be a complete academic disaster in examinations (unlike myself), university would have seemed an unlikely and foolish course for him to follow.

He told me, much later, that he had secretly resolved to find himself employment in London. A city job, with prospects, was how he described it. He had even begun to make enquiries, for the long corridors of his public school were tramped by the feet of sons of many a city gentleman. However, Marsdon, with his own plodding feet of lumpish innocence and willingness to please, was to change the course for both of us.

Ignatius Marsdon, referred to only as Marsdon by everybody, for even his parents seemed to realize how ludicrously inappropriate his first name was, was the friend that Ziggy had enticed to Cornwall for the final summer holiday. He too had left the safe portals of school and he faced the future with a frightened and hesitant blink. I hoped, as Aunt Bernice and I awaited their arrival at our usual spot by the station door, that he would be an improvement on the odious Welsh Lewis.

I was picking fretfully at the door's peeling, dull-red

paint as the train pulled in to the station, and sighed to its end-of-the line halt. Aunt Bernice rapped me sharply over the knuckles with her crochet hook and pinioned me with a beady, ferocious glance. For all her wrinkled gauntness, there was a vicious strength in Aunt Bernice's thin, prim little wrist, and my initial meeting with Marsdon, a formal shaking of hands, was marked by a smarting soreness about my knuckles. I was a great believer in fate, as the victims of resignation must be, and this did not seem to be an auspicious start.

Marsdon could not be described as an auspicious character anyway. His body was so short and so round, or rather, cylindrical, that all his clothes seemed to be both much too long for him and also much too tight. He did not look comfortably dressed at all. He had tuffeted, rust-coloured hair that stuck out awkwardly both upwards and sideways and there was a band of hot, peppery freckles across his pug-dog nose. His teeth were cruelly buck and his chin a receding dimpled mess. To add to this unprepossessing appearance he was hampered by a whistling, wheezing stammer superimposed on a sagging line in conversation that, even to me, seemed flaccid to the point of terminal decay. Despite all this, and the limp and sweaty floppiness of his hand that I shook in my thin, smarting claw, I preferred him vastly to Ziggy's previous offering of Lewis. The reason for my preference was simply that Ziggy seemed to have no more time for this peculiarly ugly, helpless creature called Marsdon, than he did for me. Until later, it was incomprehensible to me why Ziggy had been inspired to invite Marsdon to Cornwall at all.

Ziggy was still my hero; he always had been and perhaps he always would. He was the hero that I was bound to by a Gordian knot of admiration, envy and guilt. However, beyond saying that he was tall and sinewy, and that his hair was blond and bushy, rather

49

than curly, I would find it hard now to describe his physical appearance then. His presence was a dazzling, glorious reminder of my shamefully guilty intrusion on his wonderful life, and, as though he were a sacred pagan idol, I approached him with humbly lowered eyes and did not dare to look upon him directly.

The first morning of the holiday I woke to a peachy soft sky with tiny, torn shreds of faint cloud floating very high. I gazed at the pale, wispy sky through the small eyelet of my bedroom window and knew that it heralded a sun-drenched day

To my surprise Ziggy and Marsdon had risen before me and were standing in the front garden, kicking irregular trenches in the winking, granite gravel of the drive with impatient feet. This activity, according to Aunt Bernice, was particularly sinful. Throbbingly remembered, vicious reprimands had long ago kept me from riffling the gravel drive, but from the landing window Aunt Bernice, watching Ziggy and Marsdon crunching the gravel into fortifications of boredom, merely pursed her lips and kept silent. As usual Ziggy could canter freely on his luxuriously loose rein.

More surprising than the eagerly vertical awakeness of the two boys in the still-dewy garden, as yet shadowed by the tall house from the glances of the morning sun, was that they were waiting for me.

I was imperiously commanded, rather than invited, to accompany them on the day's expedition to a beach about three miles distant. Strange, surprising behaviour perhaps, but I questioned it not. Rather, I revelled in the marvel of wonderful flattery, and eagerly agreed to trudge behind them, weighted down by both the picnic and the cardboard bulkiness of the towels. To be a creature that was accepted, no, wanted, by Ziggy was a palpitating excitement indeed.

Although it was early in the morning and the sea was still lost in a sleepy haze, the beach was not deserted. Half a dozen people or more, either alone or in pairs, were wandering on the crunching sand or dabbling barefoot in the gentle splashes of the shallows, looking out to sea, to the great, wide, empty, summer-blueness of forever. We stood hesitant on the sand, and as we kicked off our shoes, feeling the damp grittiness squidging up between our toes, one of the loners, a girl, tall and elegantly slender, sauntered over to us; Samantha Crookshaw.

Her feet and ankles were bare and wetly shining from the sea, and her tumbling hair was also full of shining lights. She was wearing the sort of dress that caused Aunt Bernice to sniff with grim disgust, and she looked entirely beautiful. The enthusiasm, although chastely and beguilingly restrained, with which she greeted Ziggy demonstrated that they were far from strangers. Perhaps he and Lewis had not only been fishing for crabs last summer. Naively, I assumed that this early morning meeting on the beach was but a chance encounter, and I was flushed with shame, frustration and anger that we would have to spend the day in her beautiful company.

How foolishly, not even sweetly, innocent I was, but not for long. My role in this scenario was not again to be the butt of malicious jokes and cruel torments for the beautiful, long-limbed Samantha. Indeed, she barely acknowledged my presence; with a curt, bobbing nod to me and the same to Marsdon (although his was accompanied by a ravishing smile that made her face glow), she concentrated her charms and attentions fully on Ziggy. My part in this contrived scheme was to provide company for Marsdon while hand-in-hand Ziggy and Samantha wandered languidly along the beach. Although they wandered languidly, they did so purposefully. The far right-hand end of the beach was secluded and quiet. There was a small cove there, masked by a tumble of large boulders from the main strand of shoreline, and to this they headed. Sexual

51

innocent though I was, I was not as entirely without perception or imagination as Ziggy appeared to assume. I knew that Ziggy's muttered,

'We're going to look for something further up the beach. You two wait for us here,' was outside the realms of complete honesty.

Marsdon and I went swimming in the chill, fresh water, and although he was an ungainly, buoyant walrus of a swimmer, his efforts seemed streamlined to me, compared to those of the despised Lewis. Afterwards we sat on the beach together, uncomfortable and hesitant in each other's company on the salt-damp, striped beach towel.

I attempted to indulge in pleasant conversation. I tried to talk to Marsdon politely, and I tried to listen to his frustrating, stumbling responses, in which I'd forget the beginning of a sentence before he had finished it. Yet all the time I was trying to envisage exactly what Ziggy and Samantha were doing, just out of sight on the sands of the nearby cove.

I knew what sex was, of course. All the grim sordidity of lurid biological detail and the lyrical description of wonderful sensations and heady pleasure were not unknown concepts to me. My voracious reading had, if nothing else, allowed me to escape the prison bindings of sexual ignorance in which Aunt Bernice would rather have ensnared me, and had presumably been entrapped herself. However, like so many other things that I knew really existed – fun, love and pleasure to mention but a few – I thought that sex was something that only ever happened to other people. It was not something likely to stray into the stunted realm of myself, Ziggy and Aunt Bernice. It had never crossed my mind that our very existence was already a sign that we were irrevocably involved in at least one sexual act.

Finally, Marsdon's eyelids, pink and with curiously short, sparse, blond lashes, drooped and fluttered closed as our conversation sputtered to a feeble end, the gaps between sentences becoming ever longer, ever more unfillable. Sprawled in the sunhine, bored, perhaps, with our mutual inability to luxuriate in easy chatter, he dozed. Soon the dozing was consumed by the soft snuffles and grunts of asthmatic snoring from his pug nose. His receding jaw flopped open and his head lolled sideways. A thin strand of saliva dribbled and drooled from the corner of his mouth on to the sand. How gross and ugly we all can look in the unposed innocence of sleep, but in Marsdon this seemed to be particularly pronounced. Nevertheless, to sleep outside in the comforting warmth of the uncritical sun is a pleasant thing. I took care not to awaken Marsdon by carelessly scattering over his plump torso the tiny, slatey pebbles and slivers of shell that clung half-heartedly to my bare legs as I stood up.

The cliff top sloped gently downwards at the far end of the beach, to a grassy overhanging ledge and a vertical drop of some thirty or forty feet. The edge of the cliff overlooked the small cove and cast a deep, purple shadow over perhaps a quarter of the sand. I crawled to the cliff edge cautiously and peered down. I was careful to lie flat and not cast my own peeping shadow on to the beach. My face was pressed sideways into a clump of large red-ribbed dock leaves and I was surprised by the delicious edible fruitiness in their faint scent.

Ziggy and Samantha were not alone in the secluded cove, but although there were other people there, two or three at least, they seemed unaware of anybody. They were lying side by side on the beach, their faces locked together by their lips and their legs twisted and entwined. Ziggy's hands were thrust deep into Samantha's careless hair, and her hands were clasped behind his back. They were both fully clothed. I don't

53

know what I'd expected on this undeserted beach, but this scene rapidly became disappointing and even dull. After ten minutes of cautious staring and realizing that there was to be no progression from their present positions to anything more intriguing, I left.

Was this voyeurism? Of course it was not. It was merely a complete, unassailable curiosity. Although my devious spying on the youthful petting of Ziggy and Samantha had perhaps inspired in me strange feelings of a warm arousal lost deep inside me, in terms of sexual education they had provided me with but scanty learning material.

I had to slither backwards up to the cliff path, and this was awkward. At some points the slope was steep and there were nettle patches which were difficult to avoid in the process of retreat. I straightened up at the edge of the path, stretched briefly and slapped briskly at the nettle stings, then ran quickly back down to the beach. Guilty, I did not look back.

Marsdon was still slumbering gracelessly on the beach, so I left him and went to swim again in the cool balm of the sea. The white polyps of nettle rash, urticarial evidence of my spying borne on my arms and legs, were soothed and washed away in the gentle waves, but the water could not remove the shame of my knowledge and the guilt of my peeping. How cruel could the world be? Samantha Crookshaw, she who had kicked me with her long, elegant legs, had spat on me, and, with her jeering friends, forced me to lick spatters of her own sour urine from the seats of the school toilets, had now presented me with the ultimate torture; she lolled in the loving comfort of Ziggy's warm, strong-armed embrace, her lips seemingly fused to those of my adored, heroic brother.

The summer days drifted past, hazily, lazily, as summer days always will. Almost every single one of the days of that holiday involved my accompanying

Ziggy and Marsdon to some favoured haunt, where, minutes after we had arrived, Ziggy would slink, casually and not particularly furtively, off to a pre-arranged rendezvous with the beautiful Samantha Crookshaw. We, that is, Marsdon and myself, for quickly we had become coagulated to a single, solid, awkward, lumpish unit by Ziggy's scheming, were seldom privileged with so much as a glimmering, twinkling whisper of a glance at Samantha's shapely legs or tumbling curls. Ziggy would merely hint that he was taking himself off for a solitary, lengthy walk in a secluded and forbidden area. All we had to do was wait, as a solid, awkward, lumpish unit is so designed to do, until he returned.

It was a strange, covert, ridiculous, unspoken agreement, that could not be described as complicity. Neither myself nor Marsdon were ever consulted, or even informed, about each day's plans and thus we were never elevated to the ranks of fellow conspirators. Perhaps Marsdon really was the blind, lumbering fool that Ziggy described him as in later years, and truly did not realize how the theatre of each day unfolded, but I think not. He sometimes sighed, a soft, grunting, farmyard sigh, as Ziggy strolled nonchalantly away from us, just a little too casually for convincing authenticity. During the long hours of Ziggy's absence, it is true that Marsdon never mentioned Samantha Crookshaw nor speculated on what Ziggy might be doing, but then neither did I, and I certainly knew.

Oh, I knew all right. As Marsdon entrenched himself in his wallow of mirish sleep, as he did nearly every day (the only exceptions being those days chilled by a skittering sea wind or a spindly, pallid drizzle), I would leave him alone and stealthily seek out where Ziggy and Samantha lay.

They would invariably be discovered in the struggle of a horizontal embrace of the bruised lips and the ardent breaths of teenage desire and romantic novellas.

Their hands, hot and sticky no doubt, would be clasping and clutching at the crumpled folds of each other's scanty summer clothing and riffling eagerly, to the point of anguish, through the tumbled, tangled, glowing cascades of each other's hair.

Despite the frenzied involvement of the whole of their vehement bodies in these passionate embraces, their torsos enjoined as though crushed together by an unseen, mighty force, and their long limbs interlaced into an impossible living labyrinth; despite the searing desperation in their sighs and gasps, muffled by the fusion of their greedy mouths, they never, in the whole, long, yearning summer, progressed any further in their sexual adventures of exploration, exploitation and exultation. Ziggy told me in later years that these addictive, repeated incursions on to the borders of physical experience left him, at the end of every day, scorched by a blaze of sexual addiction and exhausting dissatisfaction; a lustful, lusting virgin. I believe him, for I watched them frequently and long.

I would lie, cheek down in the damp, mossy coolness of woodland stretches, the delicious sweetness of trifoliate wild strawberry leaves furry against my skin. Or I would sprawl, belly flat amongst the gnarled stems of springing heather of the cliff-top heathland. Or, another place, and I would be crouching low amongst the wind-rippled, shimmering green of summer meadowland, close to the cool turned earth of badger setts. I watched with the gnawing ache of guilt, disgrace and jealousy biting into my soul. Curiosity had long been satisfied, and now the voyeuristic sessions left a smarting smear of shame of some buried sexual arousal. I watched often, with cunning and deceit, but I never once saw clothing being removed, nor did I see any indication of the delicious shudder of satisfaction and completion.

Samantha Crookshaw's name was never spoken between us as Ziggy, Marsdon and I walked, or often hurried, to the rendezvous places each morning. Nor was it spoken in the violet summer dusk of our meandering home. In the presence of Aunt Bernice I quelled even the thought of Samantha, for despite all Aunt Bernice's spiritual and social blindness, in certain matters, particularly those that would involve straying from the Aunt Bernice Precepts Of Existence, she could be extraordinarily perceptive.

Thus, Ziggy's intriguing relationship with Samantha Crookshaw, about which I knew so much intimate, gasping, striving detail and which was the obvious topic of conversation for Marsdon and myself, abandoned together on sandy beaches or the rocky promontories of peninsulas, was, in an unspoken agreement, banned. Dialogue with Marsdon was wearying anyway, fractured as it was by the pitfalls of speech impediments, on his part, and conversational ignorance, on both our parts. As one, we turned to books and passed our unhurried time together in the silent companionship of reading.

No longer able to borrow books from school, I had joined, to Aunt Bernice's curtly worded disgust, the local library in town. A vast and dust-choked hall that smelt of dampness, mouse droppings and slowly rotting musty fabric, presided (if that word can be stretched a little into inappropriate usage) over by a scurrying, fragile lady, whose gentle willingness to please belied the ferret-like sharpness of her face, this room became the source of escape for both Marsdon and myself. Escape from our halting, miserable exchanges of shrunken views and an escape from the ridiculously obvious absence of Marsdon's host, Ziggy. The reason why Ziggy had bothered to bring the pathetic, lardy lump of Marsdon to Cornwall continued to puzzle me. I had not the courage nor initiative to ask him. Finally it was Marsdon who revealed for me the clue to the wisdom behind Ziggy's invitation.

Perhaps ten days or more after Ziggy and Marsdon's arrival in Cornwall, we spent another day at one of the most favoured of Ziggy's choices, the beach we had visited on the first day, where we had had our first encounter with Samantha. As usual Ziggy and Samantha were soon out of sight in the secluded cove. Excluded from our view, and hence from our thoughts and our imaginations, so we would have each other believe, by the scatter of boulders, studded with the rounded cones of ancient limpets and the mud-red, gelatinous pendules of inverted sea anemones.

It was not a sunny day. It was bleakly and briskly chilled and damply grey, and both Marsdon and I were tucked up in wool jumpers. I had thrust my knees under mine in a way that I knew Aunt Bernice deplored (she told me that I was the ruin of those misshapen garments of elderly wool), and I was deeply absorbed in my book.

It was not a good book, but it was too cold to abandon it for a swim in the frost-winking sea, and so I buried myself in it anyway. I cannot remember the title of the book, nor yet the name of the author, but much of the action, unlikely, stilted action though it was, was set in Africa. I turned the final page with satisfaction. Not the satisfaction of a fulfilling conclusion accomplished, but the unexcited satisfaction of completion of a tedious book. I put the book down carefully on the sandy shingle, although to have tossed it aside cavalierly would perhaps have been more appropriate, unruckled my knees from my sagging jumper, stretched myself and sighed. Marsdon and I had managed to slide into a routine of pretence of literary discussion, asking each other about books as we completed them and seeking recommendations.

'Good book?' Mercifully Marsdon had long since learnt to keep his sentences short where possible. It was a useful aid to the comprehension and sanity of the listener.

'No, not really. The plot was silly and so were the characters. They weren't at all like real people.' (What did I know of 'real people'?) 'I wouldn't bother to read it. The action is all over the place too. It jumps about so much you never know where you're supposed to be. London, Africa. You know what I mean?'

I felt perhaps I'd been a little snappy and curt, especially as Marsdon had thoroughly enjoyed another book by the same author. I tried to introduce a little sidetrack, a little levity, into the conversation, by adding,

'My dad died in Africa. Did you know that?' and then, 'How's your book going?'

But Marsdon had gone an uneasy shade of pinkish purple that was diffused about his face unevenly, giving him a lopsided, blotchy appearance. Perhaps I'd touched upon another forbidden subject. Perhaps he was not enjoying the book he was currently reading (I could see he was still less than halfway through it) which was one I had recommended to him. Perhaps his dad had died recently. Conversation was truly a tricky art.

Then Marsdon explained. All in a hotch-potch, mumbling, stumbling, tumbling issue of broken, falling words, slithering and sliding over and under each other, wedging themselves in his stammer and then shooting out from behind his buck teeth in a rhythm-less staccato. Emotion did not improve Marsdon's style of discourse at all. His words are much easier to paraphrase and precis than to quote.

In short, Marsdon's father had once been a friend of my own long-dead father, that one-time possessor of a pair of brown wool gloves. Marsdon's father was that very friend who had invited my father to Kenya to stay on his tea plantation, in those strange, fateful, early days of my distant past. Marsdon, a year older than Ziggy, had been four at the time.

It had been Marsdon who had found my father's convulsed body; the way in which Marsdon crunched closed his eyes, clapped his hands to his pink freckled ears and the ways his speech rolled into even less controlled paroxysms of incomprehensible grottling at this point, demonstrated that my father had been neither beautiful nor elegant in his death throes and that four-year-old Marsdon had committed my father's corpse to an unerasable region of his visual memory. Worse still, Marsdon had been accused of mischievously and wickedly placing the lithe green snake in my father's boot to begin with.

This Marsdon denied vigorously, wildly rolling not just his head, but his whole body from side to side. True he had always been interested in animals, and even at four could recognize, and perhaps handle, a boomslang. Nevertheless, he would not have dreamed of perpetrating such a terrible act. I believed him. Marsdon could not really be envisaged as the sort of small boy who would be associated with meddlesome michievousness or an evil imagination.

Now came the answer to my musings on why Ziggy had brought this awkward, lumpy youth to Cornwall with him. In return for Marsdon's trip to Cornwall with Ziggy, he had invited Ziggy to travel to Kenya with him to spend a few months (from October to February, no less) at his family home in the lush steaming green of the Kenyan Highlands. Naturally, Ziggy had seized the opportunity, especially as Marsdon's father, like myself indubitably a bearer of that wearying, tiresome load called guilt, had agreed to pay the cost of travel. I was curious to know how Aunt Bernice had taken to this proposal; it did not seem to me to be the type of venture that she would agree to support. Of course, Ziggy had not yet told her.

'But,' said Marsdon, and for once his words spilt out in a coherent line, 'but now he's eighteen, she's no longer his guardian. In fact she's no longer your guardian either – Ziggy is!' Then he delivered his final, stunning, victory blow, and perhaps because a final, stunning, victory blow was a fine and very rare thing for Marsdon, he delivered this also with a flourish of unstumbling panache,

'And Father has invited you also. You're also your father's child. You must come. You're not at school now, and Aunt Bernice can't stop you!'

Chapter Six

Marsdon Villas, Kericho, Kenya.
Dear Aunt Bernice,

We're here at last! What a terrible journey, I'm so glad it's over! We've been at Marsdon's home (Marsdon Villas) for five days now, so I thought that I'd better write to you now and let you know that we've arrived safely and give you my first impressions.

Kenya is so nice! The scenery is incredible and everything seems terribly overstated. The sky is so blue, the sun is so hot, the roads so red and dusty, and the people, the natives that is, so, so black!! The natives live in little clusters of mud huts, surrounded by hordes of filthy children, scrawny goats and rather nasty, vicious looking dogs. We haven't been close to any of these 'villages' yet, but I really rather fear that they will smell!

There's more white people around here than I imagined. Of course, there's me, Ziggy and Marsdon, then Marsdon's mother and father, who have been very nice to us. Marsdon's father has said we must call him Max! It's not his real name, I don't think, but a nickname from school that he's carried along with him throughout his life. Everybody calls him Max (apart from the natives who call him Bwana), so perhaps it won't be that difficult, although I know it does seem terribly familiar. Marsdon's mother is called Lily, but I don't presume to call her that.

Marsdon Villas is a lovely, large red brick house with a huge garden full of amazing plants. It is not in the town of Kericho, but set amongst the tea plantations that belong to Marsdon's father. I wish you could see the house, I know you would agree with me about how nice it is.

There's another family staying here too in Marsdon Villas, the Hannetts. I think they're something to do with the export of tea, but I'm not sure. They're very nice anyway, and Mr Hannett and Max spend most of their day together in the offices discussing tea. I'm getting to know the Hannetts' daughter, Arabella. She is a year older than me, and ever so beautiful, sophisticated and clever. She has been educated in England, at Cheltenham Ladies' College, and is also very nice.

There's an under-manager of the tea plantation too. He is really very nice as well. He's called Mr Ballantine, and he's from Edinburgh originally. He's not married and is quite young for such an important job. Maybe he'll marry Arabella one day. His Scottish accent isn't too hard to understand, but everyone teases him and calls him Jock or McDonald! He doesn't seem to mind.

There's also a doctor who lives quite nearby. I suppose that must be a big comfort for the Marsdon family. He's also Scottish, which is quite surprising I suppose. He's called Dr Cairns and he's from Glasgow. He and Mr Ballantine often pretend to fight about which is the better city out of Glasgow or Edinburgh! He's not married either, and is rather frightening and abrupt, but he's very nice too, although I sometimes find his accent slightly difficult to understand. All the same, nobody teases him or calls him Jock!

Dr Cairns came to dinner yesterday evening and he brought with him two young men who are staying with him. They're medical students studying at either Cambridge or Oxford, I forget which, and are spending a year here. They've been here a few months so far and already speak Swahili and are not bad at some of the tribal languages too! They're doing some sort of work with the natives, I'm not sure what, but I think

63

it's to do with parasitic worms, which sounds horrible! Nevertheless, they are very quiet and clever and also very nice. Max teased them a lot at dinner, but I wasn't sure why. It might be to do with their work, which is a little bit rude perhaps, or it might be because they're working with the natives. You know how bad and stupid at politics I am, but from what has been said, I don't think the British will be governing here much longer.

Yesterday Max, Mr Hannett and Mr Ballantine showed Ziggy, Marsdon, Arabella and me all around the tea plantations, although I suppose that Marsdon and Arabella must have seen it hundreds of times already. It was ever so nice, with acres of little bushes of tea, and each plantation has a neat little white sign in front of it with the year of planting written on in black. Max employs lots and lots of natives on the plantation, and Mr Ballantine explained that it is mostly the women who pick the tea leaves. They put it into huge baskets that they carry on their backs, and at the end of the day they weigh it to see how much they've picked. Mr Ballantine showed us the scales where the tea leaves are weighed, and a row of the baskets that they use. It was all ever so interesting and very nice.

I'm so glad you were so good about me coming here. I'm very happy, and it's very interesting. I do take care to do what Ziggy tells me, and I've offered to help about the house as you suggested, but all the housework and cooking are done by native servants! I have not forgotten all the things you told me about how I should behave, and I am remembering you in my prayers every night.

I had better end here. I hope you are well. I will write again in a fortnight. Yours lovingly, Zag.

I read through the letter twice before folding it and putting it in an envelope. I wrote Aunt Bernice's address carefully, with England in capital letters and underlined twice as she'd told me to do. In a way, I was rather proud of my letter-writing efforts. It was the sort of pallid, tame letter that I thought Aunt Bernice would like, and its liberal peppering of exclamation marks gave it just that tiny suggestion of the excitement of foreign lands. I wondered how many times I had used the word 'nice' and almost unsealed the envelope again to count. It was probably at least half a dozen times. It was an awful word at the best of times, but to describe Kenya and life here as 'nice', was surely employing an adjective that was not entirely appropriate.

I was also rather pleased by my sly inclusion of the sentence about how grateful I was that Aunt Bernice had allowed me, so graciously, to come to Kenya. Of course, ultimately, she had had no choice with Ziggy as my legal guardian. In fact, it had been the cause of much bitterness and rancour, that was kept only just beneath a simmering, smouldering surface of resignation, by Ziggy's surprising enthusiasm for me to accompany him on the trip. I suspected that he saw me as a potentially useful buffer between himself and Marsdon if any desirable alternative temptations appeared on the other side of the equator. I had obviously proved my worth with the Samantha Crookshaw episode.

I sighed and stood up. I was writing in the large plush bedroom that I had been allocated for the duration of our stay in Marsdon Villas. The room was all woodwork and soft, peachy drapery and there was a small inlaid wood desk at the window. I walked around the desk and looked out. The window overlooked the sun-drenched sloping lawn of the back garden. There was a rambling riot of wildly exuberant shrubs scattered across the grass, many of them gaudy with the showy flowers of the tropics.

Two gardeners in loose blue cotton uniforms and

blue peaked caps were standing barefoot at the furthest end of the lawn. They were chatting and laughing together and every line of their bodies reflected relaxation and a comfortable easiness. The sun glinted sharply on the blades of the machetes that hung loosely in their hands. One of the gardeners had the sleeves of his shirt rolled up and, even at that distance, I could see the bulge of his muscles under his matt black skin. He was facing me and I could see the wet pinkness of his mouth as he leaned his head backwards and laughed. As he lolled his head forward from his easy laughter he must have caught sight of me, a thin, remote, watching figure, pale and aloof, for he raised his cap towards my bedroom window, giving me a glimpse of his short neat scrolls of hair. The other gardener turned quickly towards the house then and hastily raised his cap also.

After that, the two men separated a little and bent to their work, scything down the straggles of grass that grew and festered beneath the shrubs, with long, loose sweeps of their machetes. I felt a snarl of jealousy gripping somewhere deep inside me. If only I could be as relaxed and carefree and happy as these gardeners, I thought. If only I was not tied to the stresses and cares of foolish convention. I did not consider my thoughts to be naive; they seemed to be wise thoughts to me then. There was no time to ponder jealously now, however, on the easy and relaxed life that I perceived to be the luck of these gardeners, for it was teatime. Teatime was a conventional stress of the Kenyan colonial existence to which I felt bound.

Afternoon tea was always served promptly at 3.30 p.m. in Marsdon Villas. If it was not an afternoon of the deluging tropical rain that keeps the Kenyan Highlands so lush and green, then tea was served on the front lawn. The front lawn lay just beyond the vine-draped veranda where, I imagined, for nobody had told me, my father had long ago had his fatal encounter with the boomslang coiled in his riding boot. As I crossed the drawing room to the French windows, which opened on to the veranda, I could hear the chill British clinking of bone china cups on bone china saucers, an accompaniment to the even chillier British clinking of bone china conversation. I was late.

There were a lot of people around for tea that afternoon. Marsdon's mother, Lily, was fretting at the two houseboys, in their starched white uniforms with their red braid trims and gold buttons. They were not pouring the tea fast enough. Ziggy, Marsdon and Arabella, however, had already got their cups of tea. They were sitting together in a small and excluding circle with the two medical students, Andrew and Richard.

I could never remember which of the pair was Andrew and which was Richard, and most of the time it didn't seem to matter. They were so earnest and eager, those two medical students, both with their quick, intelligent, gooseberry eyes and sharp, beak-like noses. They had incredibly well-scrubbed hands with pinkly shining fingernails and they seemed always to smell slightly of soap and Dettol. They spent most of their days in the local native villages, weighing the babies and younger children in a sort of dangling contraption that reminded me of farmyards. They also collected samples of faeces and urine in carefully numbered vials and bottles, which they mixed and sieved and spent many hours examining under a microscope in Dr Cairns's office.

I felt sure that they must have a lot of fascinating stories. Perhaps they did, but they were bottled up in formalin and never displayed. Instead they had a stock of lavatorial slapstick jokes and anecdotes, which they would sometimes mutter to Ziggy, Marsdon, Arabella and me, but mostly they were terribly prim and serious about their work. The way that Ziggy and Marsdon

67

were sniggering and Arabella improving her beauty with a graceful blush as I approached the tea party, suggested that yet another tale of a curiously misplaced sample bottle was being related. Although far from unpleasant, Andrew and Richard would have been better described as dull, earnest and tedious, rather than 'nice'.

I'd described most people as 'nice' in my letter to Aunt Bernice. What about Arabella? Was she nice? I didn't know, for she was totally inaccessible to me. Her tall, fragrant beauty, flowerlike and fragile, distanced us immediately. Her gentle chimes of conversation, mingled with peals of singing laughter, humbled and ashamed me, and left me speechless with bitter envy and regret. Ziggy was clearly entrapped by her honey charm, but unlike Samantha Crookshaw she dangled him at arm's length, never allowing him close enough for even a fingertip touch, and making it clear that young Mr Ballantine, the plantation under-manager, was her hero.

Mr Ballantine – Arabella called him Tom or Tommy – was good-looking in a rugged, nondescript, inexplicable type of way. His blue eyes seemed to be orientally slanted, and they were lost in the shadows of tired, overworked bags. Uneven spikes of coarse black hair emerged from his flaring nostrils. His mouth seemed to be too big for his face and his forehead was sleepily creased and anxiously furrowed. Nevertheless, the features slotted together well and made a charming, pleasant, honest face, and his nature was kind, polite and courteous. He lived a mile or so further into the plantation in a white bungalow, wrapped in vines, and with a long, shady veranda. He lived with two native servants: a woman who cooked his meals, cleaned the house and did his washing and a man who tended his sprawling garden and drove and cleaned his ancient battered car. His servants didn't wear uniform and he seemed to treat them more as friends than employees. I could see why Arabella had selected him as the recipient for all her directed charms and I already worshipped him too. However, I had no charms to direct at him and merely watched from an embarrassed, shy and humble distance.

As I joined the tea-party gathering, Mr Ballantine was, as usual, engrossed in talk with Max. He had his tea cup gripped in his right hand, while his left hand was waving the fragile saucer about in the air in an animated and energetic explanation. Max was standing very still and very quiet, listening to him, his head of shining thick white hair leaning to one side. He seemed almost patronizing in his owl-like, lopsided demeanour, allowing the young Tom Ballantine (Mr Ballantine was just thirty years old, whereas Max was fast approaching sixty) to have his say. Doubtless, however, he was listening carefully, for he knew Mr Ballantine was an excellent under-manager, and Max's own fine judgement and attention to detail had made this plantation one of the most successful in the whole of East Africa.

Five other people were also at the gathering. Dr Cairns was there, red moustache bristling angrily. He had walked a little apart from the group and was looking accusingly into a clump of jasmine. Its scent was barely discernible in the mid-afternoon heat, for jasmine waits for the short, tropical, violet dusk to fall before it whispers out its seductive potency.

There were also a man and woman that I had not seen previously. Aged in their mid-fifties and clearly a married couple, both rather a portly pink and rotundly complacent, they were helping themselves to something creamy and delicious-looking from the cakestand and murmuring trivially to the Hannetts, Arabella's mother and father. The Hannetts were also exploring the possibilities of the sumptuous cakestand and I wondered if I should make a mention of this platter of delicious and gooey sweetness in my next letter to

Aunt Bernice. It was the sort of wasteful, luxurious frippery that she detested and despised. In Marsdon Villas, however, it was regarded as a humble essential, in that it was not regarded at all.

Max noticed me out of the corner of his quick, kindly eye, still tinged with the guilt of my father, as I hesitated on the edge of the party.

'Zag, my dear, where have you been? We have all started without you. Look, there are no chairs left at all. Lily dearest, when you have finished supervising the tea-pouring, please do call someone to bring some more chairs. Poor old Zag here and young Tom, and of course Dr Cairns have all got to stand up. Oh, and I need a chair too, and so do you, so that's five more chairs needed.'

'Tea? Ma'am, tea?' One of the houseboys was looking at me enquiringly out of his brown, dog eyes. I noticed the whites were a dusky yellow, as though stained with cigarette smoke.

'Of course she wants tea, boy. Now do hurry up and pour it. I hope you heard what the bwana said about chairs too.' Lily, Marsdon's mother, sounded petulant and crossly anxious. The daughter of a Liverpudlian cobbler, I rather fancied she was still in awe of the pretensions of Kenyan colonial society, and snapped at it like an over-fed lap dog.

I was still not accustomed to grown-up men, sometimes quite elderly men, with grizzled white hair and faces lined with their lives, being called 'boy', even if they were black. I smiled as winningly as my mean, pinched-up face could manage at the two servants, the one pouring tea and the other bearing it to the drinkers with humble tread. Neither seemed perturbed by Lily's bossy petulance, but they smiled back at me, and the one who poured the tea winked. Lily, Arabella, Mrs Hannett and the unknown lady eating creamy gateau sniffed and tutted. I winced. I had already been told several times by Lily not to smile at the servants.

'You see, Zag dear,' she had said, 'if you get familiar with them, they take advantage. I am not being cruel. I speak from experience.' She had stressed the word experience with the sad, weary sigh of the unappreciated martyr. 'They are nice people, but they aren't clever and they are cunning. They easily get cheeky and sloppy. Just like naughty children, if you give them an inch, they take a mile. So, no familiarity please. You do see, don't you?'

I had said yes, of course, although really I had not been able to see at all. Aunt Bernice had, at least, not planted any racism inside me in my upbringing, probably because coloured people never crossed our path in Cornwall, rather than due to an ethic of racial equality. I continued to be forgetful and would smile at the servants, and be pleased by the friendly smiles and winks and nods that I received in return.

Here I was being sinfully familiar yet again, and I shrank inside myself quickly, stung by the irritated barbs of female, white-skinned scorn. However, today Lily had determined to be kind and friendly to this stupid, foolish, ugly waif who was myself, and as I sat down in the white wicker chair that the houseboy brought out for me (I was careful not to smile at him, or even look him in the eye), she leant forward and patted me on the knee.

'Zag, I must introduce you to some very dear friends of ours, Mr and Mrs Frobisher. Mr Frobisher works down in Nairobi, he does very important government work which is much too clever for us to understand. They are just up for the weekend and are staying in our famous Kericho Tea Hotel. Arnold, Julia, this is Zag, the daughter of a very dear friend of ours.' At this point Lily rolled her eyes dramatically towards the left-hand end of the veranda behind us. I suppose she thought that I was too blind and foolish and young to notice. She continued her introductions after a pause that was just long enough to weigh significantly

71

in the warm air, 'and Sigmund, Ziggy, here is her brother.'

'This is your first time in Kenya then?' asked Mr Frobisher, turning his plump, bland, self-satisfied face towards me. Why was it that everyone, the Hannetts, Mr Ballantine, Dr Cairns, Richard, Andrew, everyone, had started off their attempts at conversation with that same superior enquiry of patronage? This time Lily answered for me.

'Oh, yes. Neither Ziggy nor Zag have been outside The Old Country before. I don't believe Zag has ever even travelled outside Cornwall, have you dear?'

Why, oh why, did they always refer to Britain as 'The Old Country'? It was so chummily nauseating. I did not ask, however, and instead answered,

'I spent a week in London last winter, but that's all.'

'And do you know what she did in London?' This was Ziggy chiming in now, Andrew and Richard having presumably exhausted their tales of shit and pee for the day. 'She spent all week talking to the widow of an Irish labourer in her kitchen. Her chance to go to all the museums and art galleries and things, but no! Zag preferred to stay gossiping in the kitchen!'

Ziggy could be very harsh sometimes. Arabella sniggered behind a white lace handkerchief and arched her fine delicate eyebrows disdainfully over her periwinkle eyes. Andrew, or possibly Richard, tried to disguise his snigger with a cough. Lily, Mrs Hannett and Mrs Frobisher gave polite little laughs of amazement that tinkled with the china tea cups.

'What a funny little child you are, Zag,' said Lily. When you are a full sixteen years old it is hard to be called a little child. To be called a funny little child is harder yet. I flushed.

'I LIKE kitchens and I LIKED Mrs O'Cavanagh,' I said, trying to sound adultly annoyed rather than childishly irritable. Dr Cairns came unexpectedly to my aid,

'I like kitchens too, although I don't generally like landladies. The former are often warm, cosy and comfortable and the latter anything but.'

There was a general friendly laugh, and Mr Ballantine and Max also joined in. Their voices sounded kind and supportively paternal.

'Yes, I like kitchens too. Landladies fall into two categories; either ogres or angels. You were lucky to get one of the second type as they are definitely a minority.'

'Zag, please do feel free to go into the kitchen any time you like. I'm sure the servants will be only too pleased to chatter away to you endlessly, and do even less work than usual.'

'If that's possible,' his wife added sourly.

Rotund Mr Frobisher brought the conversation pompously back to its head.

'So neither of you,' and he bracketed Ziggy and me together in a swerving roll of his protuberant eyes, 'neither of you have ventured to this mighty land and infamous colony before? Tell me, what do you think of it? I love to hear the views of new and unwearied eyes.' He put his fat smug hand to his round bald forehead in a gesture of mock exhaustion.

Ziggy was a good responder to these sorts of questions, and we'd heard enough of them in the last five days. I felt extremely weary of obligingly being the ignorant novice, but Ziggy always answered with zest and innocent enthusiasm. He gave the sort of reply that the questioner wanted. A simple background on which to display the depths of experience and hard-earned wisdom.

'Oh! It's wonderful here, fantastic. So exotic and so exciting. Everything seems so primitive and unexplored and natural out there. Then, in an incredible contrast, there's this house, Marsdon Villas, and cultured people like yourselves.' Ziggy flourished his hand in a dramatic, sweeping, all-embracing gesture.

The eloquence of his answers was certainly improving with practice. 'It all seems so amazing. The weather is so wonderful too, and then there's the plants and the birds, and animals of course. Wild animals, not that we've seen any yet, and there's so many other things too. I think I could never grow bored here.'

It was the sort of answer that the all-knowing expatriate community fostered and loved.

'Oh, it's good to hear the unjaded views of credulous youth, isn't it?' laughed Mr Frobisher. 'Don't you think, Max? Eh, Mr Hannett? Dr Cairns?'

It was Mrs Hannett who answered, however; the usual warning reply to remind us of their years of wisdom.

'Don't be deceived, Ziggy, that's all we ask. We all came to Kenya, many years back,' a tinkling, self-conscious laugh at that point, 'with those innocent hopes and thoughts too. But now . . .' and she left her familiar, cautionary answer hanging in midair. A mystery of hard-earned wisdom and experience.

They always proffered us these hopeless, unfinished, dangling warnings. Warnings of what, I wondered. Of boredom and tedium? Of mistrust, small talk and bitterness? Of petty rivalries and querulous enmities? Probably all those and more, much more. Small, foolish quarrels derived and bred in narrow, selfish existences, festering in the humid heat of the tropical sunshine. To leave the sentence hanging in that irritating, tempting manner left room for more intriguing reasons to be suspected for the gloomy shaking of the head.

'And Zag, how do you find this Kenya of ours? How do you compare it with, what, fifteen years in Cornwall and one week in a kitchen in London?' Mr Frobisher certainly knew the art of smug and patronizing condescension. I was hesitant in my answer.

'It's very nice.' There was that awful, insipid word again. No other word could be found. What did I know

74

of Kenya? Five days of living in this affluent little Britain, with delicious food and uniformed, softly padding servants. Five days of strolling idly in a heat-soaked garden, crackling with boldly chattering greedy birds and splashed with vulgarly-bright tropical flowers. Five evening meals of starched white tablecloths, glinting silver cutlery and the light sparkling back from the highly polished glasses, with conversations about The Old Country and problems with natives. Five days of feeling compressed by my dismal lack of sophistication, education and experience.

Oh, it had been Kenya all right, but I knew there must be more to this country than that. Outside the plush comfortable confines of the world of Marsdon Villas and the tea plantations there was a Kenya that I had only glimpsed. A Kenya of trickling woodsmoke and strong-scented animal dung. A Kenya of crying babies suckled openly for comfort and solace, and raucous singing and raucous fighting. A Kenya of round mud homes with thatched roofs and dark, beckoning doorways. A Kenya of mud-red tracks and footpaths that led onwards and forever to places I didn't know and probably never would. How could I possibly describe this unknown country? I repeated what I'd said before more firmly.

'It's very nice.' Nice meant nothing at all, and I knew nothing at all. I wondered if any of them realized that I was using nice as my code word for a confession, an admission, of ignorance. I rather doubted it.

It was time for Mr and Mrs Frobisher to leave. They would have to bath and change their clothes before dinner in the Tea Hotel. These people seemed to be drifting, no, waddling, no, worse still, being chauffeured from meal to meal. Their plump smugness was not a thing to be wondered at, at all. I was not sorry to see them leave. Mrs Frobisher kissed me, or rather made a strange, smacking, whistling noise with her lips about an inch from my right ear, a polite non-kiss. Mr Frobisher, Max called him Arnie, which deflated his corpulent, governmental dignity somewhat, kissed me wetly on the lips. His breath smelt of alcohol and festering decay, and his dry mottled skin smelt of expensive scent. They would be back for dinner the following night.

'A good, British, Sunday dinner,' was how Lily put it. Mrs Frobisher (she was too saggingly, dumpily plump even to be thought of as Julia, a name designed for svelte elegance) had sighed,

'Oh, how wonderful; a dinner to remind us of The Old Country.'

I was unable to stop my face sliding into a contemptuous grimace at her words. A private revenge for her earlier smug superiority over Ziggy and me. I did not imagine that anyone would notice my nose and lips twitching derisively, but there was a burst of chuckling from my left. I jumped guiltily, and both Mr Ballantine and Dr Cairns sent Scottish conspiratorial winks in my direction.

Sunday morning saw our faces carved to the passive tranquillity of marble saints. No grimaces, no conspiratorial winks or nudges on this day of worship. A faint, tinny chiming, rising and falling in distant undulation over the tea plantations, languidly rolling through the warm steaminess of the gold-trickled dawn had woken me. From my bedroom window I could see that it had rained hard during the night. There was a messy, muddy, trampled puddliness at the bottom of the sloping back lawn, and the large drooping leaves of the nameless tropical shrubs glinted wetly in the first streaks of sunlight. Nevertheless, by breakfast time the morning sun was already baking hard the sodden red clay soil, and there was the warm, heavy smell of drying vegetation in the air.

It seemed to be a tradition in Marsdon Villas to detest the colonial Kenyan breakfasts; they were so unlike anything that you would ever be served in The Old Country. Fat succulent slices of bulbously ripe, freshly-picked pawpaw, its slightly cloying sweetness honed to an exquisite deliciousness by the biting juice squeezed from the tiny sharp limes which were served cut into thick yellow-green wedges. Coffee, ground that morning from the smooth roasted beans and served from a huge white, china pot, very black. Mrs Hannett had whispered that she pined for the sizzle and smack of frying eggs and bacon, and Lily had once mentioned, very wistfully, black pudding. It seemed strange to me that this sultry, heavy heat should make them crave the solid weight of a greased breakfast. I suppose that it wasn't really the breakfast that they were pining for.

Mr and Mrs Hannett left the breakfast table quickly to sort out what they ambiguously described as 'bed linen problems'. Ziggy, Arabella, Marsdon, his parents and I lingered on, eating with lazy ease. Max even called for another slice of the detested pawpaw.

Ziggy, too, had been awoken by the early morning bell chimes. Unlike me, however, he was not too foolish and scared to ask about them.

Max was plainly proud of his display of religious morality. He had built the small stone church for the plantation residents and workers as one of his first priorities. Or, rather, he had overseen the building of the church. It had been, for some reason, an awkward building in its construction, and three of the labourers, no less, had met messy and untimely ends while working on it. Two had slipped and fallen from its walls, and another had been hit on the head by a badly handled wooden beam. Their bodies had been buried beneath the church. Max had bought three small brass plates and had each inscribed with the name of one of the labourers, and these had been screwed into the stone floor of the church above where the bodies had been interred. This had been seen as a profoundly magnanimous gesture by everybody, and much applauded. True, they were in an obscure, dark back-pantry type area of the church, but to have three natives buried under the church at all was kindness indeed. Max's reputation for liberal generosity towards the natives had spread.

'You see,' said Max, pointing at Ziggy with the end of his silver fork, on which was speared a juicy fat chunk of orange-yellow pawpaw, 'in the bible it says that we are all equal in the eyes of God. You know what that means? White, black, even goddamn yellow, we are all equal. I feel that means we should all have the chance to pray equally. What say you, Ziggy? Hmmm, Zag?'

We both nodded silently. The houseboy stood darkly and impassively in his starched white uniform next to the sideboard, ready to pour more coffee as soon as it was requested. His inward-gazing brown eyes offered no opinions. Lily bent her own eyes meekly downwards to the remains of her breakfast pawpaw. It was implied in her gesture that she too, virtuously, agreed with Max.

Neither Marsdon nor Arabella appeared to be listening to Max. Arabella was gazing out of the window towards the drive. There was a look of studied boredom in her beautiful eyes and in the pout of her lips, but I knew that she was watching out impatiently for the arrival of Mr Ballantine. Marsdon was gazing helplessly at Arabella. How foolish and blind of me not to have realized previously that it was not only Ziggy who had succumbed, sliding under the hypnotic honey tendrils of her feminine charms and beauty.

Max was still talking about his church and of his kind and exemplary magnanimity to the poor heathen blacks. His voice was raised a little, as though in declamation.

'So, that church that I built, that church that cost me so much in my time, my labour, and, let's face it, my money, that church is not just for us. We are all equal in the sight of God; I know I have said it once and I say it again. Therefore I have said, no, insisted, that every man, woman or child, black or white, living or working on this plantation, attends that church of mine every Sunday.'

Max was growing quite heated with his pronouncements. His face had reddened and his blue eyes sparked. Nobody had raised a word in disagreement, but Max's voice seemed to suggest that he was embroiled in a passionate argument. I noticed a muscle twitching in his cheek, next to his left eye. I felt Ziggy was being very daring to ask a question at this point.

'So why were the bells ringing so early this morning?' Max slammed his fist down on to the table. The cups jumped in their saucers with a nervous, clattering chatter of bone china clinking. The shining silver cutlery hummed with the reverberation. The houseboy sprang forward with the coffee pot held aloft like a victory shield, but nobody wanted any. Arabella and Marsdon shot their dreamy eyes into focus on Max's flushed, twitching face. He had certainly grabbed the attention of the breakfast-table audience. He lowered his voice to a hiss, as sibilant and coiled as any boomslang, and waved his fork at Ziggy again.

'Why do you think, my boy? Come on, look at it. Do you think we're all going to crowd in there together? Do you think Arabella is going to sit squeezed between two runny-nosed stinking black kids or next to some unshaven, spitting, revolting negro labourer? Of course not! Do you think I'd let Lily, or your sister here, in with that seething horde of black-fleshed humanity? No. We must strive to balance God's equality with practicality.' His voice returned to its normal jovial tones, and his face resumed its usual healthy unflushed leathery tan. The muscle in his cheek had stopped twitching. He speared another chunk of pawpaw on his fork and bit into it.

Lily signalled to the houseboy to pour more coffee. Arabella and Marsdon returned to their separate, hopeful, moist-eyed gazing; Marsdon at Arabella, and Arabella out of the window. Max speared another chunk of pawpaw and gulped down a mouthful of the snapping coffee.

'First service for all the labourers and their families. That's at six. Second service for any house staff, and office staff too, clerks and that. Not just the house staff at the Villas here, but young Mr Ballantine's couple too. That allows them to get back to their duties good and early, with no time wasted. Third service for any of the natives that didn't belong in either of the first two categories, or who missed their service for some reason. That's not encouraged of course, because it encourages laziness, and God knows they're lazy enough already. Then there's a break while the church people have breakfast, and also the church is swept out and cleaned. I can tell you, my boy, after all those unwashed niggers sitting in there, it needs a good scrub. Then it's our turn, by which time, of course, it's a reasonable and civilized hour.' He chuckled with pleasure; he clearly thought that he had dealt rather cleverly with God's tricky equality business. I was enboldened by Max's quick return to an easy, friendly chattiness, but I still felt I was being very brave to put forward a question.

'And is it the same person who takes all the services? And is it a white man or a native?'

Max put his fork down and looked me very straight in the eye. How blue his eyes were. They cut into me like steel, like an ice wind. I realized I had asked the wrong question. Why did I always have to make these stupid, blundering, clumsy mistakes? His voice, when he answered after a pause lasting a sickening eternity, was calm and even, but the jovial tones were drained

80

away leaving an icy chill. It was a more frightening voice than his previous blustering roar or taut hiss.

'Do you think that I'd allow some ignorant native to preach at me? Who do you think I am, Zag? Would I dare, do you imagine, to lower the tone of God's word like that? Our vicar is Father Samuel Mannering. He attends all the services, but those for our black brothers are usually given by the good Mannering's native helper, Jacob. At both Christmas and Easter Mannering takes all the services. Is there anything else you would care to know?'

Although it was I who had asked this somehow terrible question, it was Ziggy, rather than me, that Max addressed. His flat, cold, harsh voice challenged Ziggy to dare to ask a question. Father Samuel Mannering was obviously not a popular man with Max. Out of the corner of my eye (for like a frightened rabbit I could not move my head, my neck seemed to be set into position, facing Max's grim, set countenance), I saw Marsdon looking at Ziggy with anxious desperation, pleading with him not to continue. Rolling my eyes in the opposite direction I could see an equally pleading expression etched between the wrinkles and the folds of sagging jaw on Lily's face. Only Arabella seemed detached from the chilling blasts of forbidden and icily furious mystery.

'No. Thank you, sir. Max, I mean.' Ziggy's voice was very small and somewhat distant. It seemed to be projected cautiously from the very back of his skull. I wondered if he had been such a frail, diminutive character in the bluster of his school. Such a thought did not diminish my worship of him; it emphasized anew how ignorantly remote from his elevated plane of existence I was. There was an expanding silence of concentric circles imploding around the breakfast table. Even the houseboy seemed to have stopped breathing.

The crunching rattle of tyres on the drive jerked us

into action like pistol shots. Never had pistol shots been so welcome. A tiny sigh escaped from Arabella, but I doubt that anyone heard it but me. Attention was still focused on Max. He squealed back his chair roughly, jerkily, and flung himself out of the room to go and meet Mr Ballantine. For the first time I noticed the slight roll in Max's gait. He had a limp in his right leg. We all stood up then, and, apart from Arabella, seemed to draw a communal deep breath. Marsdon was trying to speak to Ziggy with desperate rapidity. An urgent message that stumbled and fell, collapsing futilely in his stammer and amongst his buck teeth. Lily poured her words with an easy fluidity over her poor son's stuttering.

'Zag, Ziggy, please try not to mention Father Mannering to my husband again. You see how it upsets him. He is really not a very welcome figure here at all, but he is the only qualified person available to take the services.'

She shrugged helplessly, hopefully. I nodded. Her anxious, pleading statement was sufficient for me, although hardly a satisfactory explanation. Aunt Bernice had tutored me thoroughly in the precepts of unquestioning obedience without reasoning, and the theory that all explanations were necessarily embarrassing. Ziggy had not received such instruction. The whole of his body was arched into a question mark. His whole face and expression shrieked out 'why?'. Lily flushed.

'Father Mannering's relations with his native assistant, Jacob, have caused us, and particularly Max, some . . .' and she paused here, briefly damping her crackled lips with the pink tip of her curiously young-looking tongue. (It was as though she were selecting the appropriate word by taste. Perhaps she was being careful to choose a word that was not too revealing.) '. . . worry.'

The door opened then, and Mr Ballantine, in a dark

grey suit and a lettuce-crisp shirt, strode cheerily into
the nervous room. His unflustered and unworried
stride seemed to clear some lurking and evil poison
from the air.

'Good morning ladies, Ziggy, Marsdon. Still at
breakfast? Why, Father Mannering will be getting
impatient soon.'

Max had followed Mr Ballantine into the room. He
did not flinch or react in the slightest to the careless
hurling of the worrying minister's name into the
strangled breakfast air. Instead he slapped both Ziggy
and me boisterously across the shoulders.

'They have been keeping me talking, have these
two,' he said. There was his usual kindly, beaming
friendliness in both the slap and his voice. Already the
ice seemed to have become even less than a thawed
memory; perhaps only a frozen dream. For some
reason only seeing again the shadowy limp, that I had
failed to observe at all until that morning, convinced
me that there really were strong currents of dangerous
chill flowing invisibly beneath Max's benign and
jovial surface.

The church was small, as Max had said it would be,
but rather than the quaint grey stone I had imagined,
its walls were cleanly whitewashed. Mr Ballantine
explained to me that this was to add to the coolness
inside by reflecting the sun's burning heat. Arabella
sniffed; I was being very ignorant. Inside the air was
cool and softly dim, and there were sprays of nameless
white tropical flowers on the narrow window sills and
in the corners. Motes of dust danced on the rays of
sunlight which slipped into the church, and there was
a sweet, clean, aniseedy smell that reminded me of the
sea-salt-swept wild fennel of Cornish hedgerows. I
wondered if my father had prayed here and been
reminded of his distant home, his lost, sad wife, his
golden son and the daughter that he never knew.

The sermon was short and uninspired, but I stared with a greedy fascination at the balding minister and his soft-stepped, pool-eyed native assistant, both clothed in their long-sleeved ankle-length white cotton gowns, hoping to discern some air of evil mystery. Father Mannering, however, looked ordinary and plain-featured – the sort of face that is instantly forgettable. His assistant, Jacob, had the usual subservient, graceful air that seemed to envelop nearly all the natives in the presence of their employers, although obsequious grovelling was unusual. In short, neither the appearance of Father Mannering or Jacob, nor the atmosphere of the church betokened either mystery or evil. My lurking desire for the revelation of corruption in pious authority was frustrated.

There were short prayers in the service begging for all the usual boring Christian virtues, and forgiveness for not possessing them anyway. Also we prayed for The Old Country, and I was disappointed that the unmentionable Father Mannering should also use this nauseous terminology for Britain. We knelt on the cold hard stone floor to pray, and glancing slyly up, I saw that Max alone remained seated in his dark wood pew. His face was encased in his large veined leathery hand, with his shaggy white eyebrows peeking over his thumb. I wondered if his distaste for the minister prevented him from kneeling before him, or was it merely his leg troubling him? Throughout the dull intonation of our humble beseechings I amused myself by wondering what he could have done to his leg. I considered lions and tigers (although I knew we were on the wrong continent for the latter). Native spears, crocodiles, elephants, even a hippopotamus could cause problems for an unwary leg. There were so many delightful, fascinating possibilities in this unknown and promising land. Much later I was disappointed to discover that Max had long suffered from gout in his right leg.

Then there was a hymn, an old favourite, and somewhat inappropriate, but I was proud to hear how our unaccompanied voices seemed to swell and rise up, filling the church with a yearning gratitude for the Rock of Ages. Max and Mr Ballantine sang out with an uninhibited vigour, and Mr Hannett, Ziggy, and the two medical students, and even Marsdon, rumbled satisfyingly behind them. The female voices of Lily, Mrs Hannett, Arabella and me seemed to be lifted on buoyant waves too, and Mrs Hannett appeared to have both musical pretensions and training, for she included trills and cadences in plaintive harmony. Only Dr Cairns, I noticed, was not singing. He was standing next to me, and although his narrowly separated pale blue eyes bored into the words printed in the musty hymn book, and although his ferocious moustache wobbled and fretted menacingly as his narrow mouth shaped the words, he made not a sound. It seemed an improbable show of cowardice from him; a sour, dour Scot seemed unlikely to be a silent and timorous faker. Nor did he join in our final song, a rousing chorus of the National Anthem. As we soared up its chanting, ugly tune, I wondered if the natives, champing restlessly in the trappings of colonialism, also had to sing this monstrous ditty every Sunday.

We filed slowly and primly out of the church. Father Mannering and his assistant Jacob stood in the shaded doorway serenely waiting for us. Jacob bowed his head in a deferential but mechanical nodding as each of us passed. I looked down too and I saw that his feet were bare on the cold floor. His black toes, which seemed as old and gnarled as wet tree roots in a rainy wood, were thickly splayed, and his toenails brightly, palely pink and innocently defenceless. I saw this in just the leisurely blinking of my two unhurried steps that walked me past him. Jacob's feet were clutched into my visual memory for ever. Then I was shaking the long-fingered, damp, thin, freckled hand of Father

Mannering, as Dr Cairns walking in front of me had done.

'Bless you, my child,' he said. His voice, as throughout the service, was bland, uninspired and dull, but I was embarrassed by the unknown, unimaginable atrocities performed by himself and Jacob – atrocities that had snapped at our breakfast – and I glanced only briefly up into his face. I did not meet his eyes, but I saw them. They were bland, uninspired and dull too. A dirty, murky, muddy grey in colour, they were looking blankly at nothing. It was evident that his blessing had been the fluttering passing of a mechanical verbal reflex. I dropped my eyes quickly, and mumbled 'Thank you.' I doubt whether he heard me.

Outside the mute shadowiness of the church door, I blinked in the blue-white dazzle of the Kenyan midday. The glaring brightness, such a contrast to the soft, dim interior of the church, brought tears spontaneously to my eyes. I paused in my steps and raised my hand to shade my eyes. The whitewashed church seemed to be shimmering almost viciously, reflecting back the stabbing light of the sun. The noon heat also pierced into me instantly, engulfing me in a torrid swelter. I could feel unhurried thick globules of sweat rising in my armpits and on my limp wrists, and slowly beading down my back.

My fellow members of the congregation had not paused for idle chatter after the sanctified silence of church, nor had they waited to congratulate the vicar on his tedious sermon. They had not, however, headed, as I thought they would, straight for where the cars were waiting for us, glinting hotly under a shimmer of red dust on the dirt road. They had gathered instead in a sweat-sticky, pale-clothed huddle in the angle of the glutinous euphorbia hedge that marked the boundaries of the church's holy influence.

I walked towards them, a dozen or so slow and careful steps, for the sultry heat seemed to be sucking the fluid life out of me at every movement. My hair appeared to be stuck down to my scalp in a tightening, skull-cracking helmet. I realized with a damply slapping shock of fear and shame that I felt horribly ill and nauseous. My abdomen felt tightly stretched and balloon-like, as distended as any of those belonging to the grubby dark shrieking children who had run, barefoot in clouds of red dust, after the cars on the way to the church. I could feel a threatening liquid burbling in the depths of my unsure stomach, and I could picture its contents as a green and scummy bubbling slime. I closed my eyes briefly, and there were white soft-focus circles skidding hectically sideways behind my eyelids. I opened my eyes, and a drearily blurred Marsdon stepped aside in front of me. I took a wobbling, tentative half-step forward.

There was a grey stone, about two foot high and one foot wide, in the ground by the euphorbia hedge, and a small wooden cross, slightly lopsided and painted white. Everyone seemed to be looking either at the stone or at me; I could feel their gloating, contemptuous eyes gnawing into me with the sultry, whore-like scorn of rank and loathsome rats. I blinked, a deep, heavy blink, and forced my achingly onerous eyes in a weary roll to focus on the stone. It seemed to be so important. There was my father's name engraved on the stone, and a date, and a simple message, 'Rest In Peace'.

I lurched towards the stone, seeking its grey solidity for support. I felt my legs crumbling and I was on my knees in the bristles of soft dry spiky grass, and my hands, slithering, clutching talons, pulled at my father's headstone. I wondered, vaguely and distantly, if they thought that I was praying, perhaps for his soul, perhaps for mine.

I could feel the tightening band of sweat-soaked constriction around my forehead, and the white balls now swung and swivelled before my wide-open,

87

staring eyes. The centres of these hazy circles bulged and melted into a dull purple. Time was either hurtling forwards in an uncontrolled ricochet, or it had ceased entirely, and I saw each of my pained movements, drenched in odious sudor, as precise and infinitely prolonged. I leaned forward to rest my perspiration-glazed forehead against the rough, scraping reality of the stone, searching for a steadiness which would control the lurching dances of the blurred spheres.

I felt again the churning scum seething in my stomach. I felt it rise, as though boiling over, to my throat in hideous green, sliming, golloping dollops. I didn't attempt to choke back the bout of guilt and shame engulfing me, but in futile submission opened my mouth and retched and retched and retched. To my weary surprise the globular trail of glutinous, viscous vomit that drooled down my father's tombstone was not the stewed-spinach green of my imagination, but a vile and fulvous pawpaw orange.

Chapter Seven

Marsdon Villas, Kericho, Kenya.
Dear Aunt Bernice,

You will probably be surprised to read that I am writing this from my bed in Marsdon Villas. The day after I wrote my last letter to you, I was very ill. Nobody seems to be quite certain of what it was, but Dr Cairns (I wrote to you about him in my last letter) thought it was probably something I'd eaten, combined with the heat and perhaps even a touch of the dreaded malaria. I'm much better now, so please don't worry, and Dr Cairns has said that I am allowed out of bed tomorrow morning.

Meanwhile, Ziggy, Arabella and Marsdon are out all the time doing terribly interesting and exciting things with Max and Mr Ballantine or sometimes Mr Hannett. However, Lily, Marsdon's mother, has very kindly lent me a whole set of Dickens, so you can imagine that I am entertained very well, despite seeing little of anyone here.

The servants bring me my meals in bed, and have also been very kind to me. All the same it will be nice to be allowed to get up. The evening of the day I fell sick I missed a dinner party given by Max and Lily to which all the white people hereabouts came, including Mr and Mrs Frobisher who were up from Nairobi for the weekend, staying in a very grand and famous hotel in Kericho called the Tea Hotel. I had met them at afternoon tea the day before, they were very nice, and I believe that Mr Frobisher is something rather important in the Government.

Still, I can't complain. I know that I am ever so lucky to be here at all, and I am sure to see the Frobishers another time. They come up to the Highlands quite often, as, although it is presently very hot here, the air is very much fresher than in Nairobi. At least when I am out of bed tomorrow I will not be being such a nuisance to everybody at Marsdon Villas. I will end here. I apologize for the brevity of this letter, but since I last wrote, being ill has occupied much of my time! I have even had to miss church. Nevertheless, I have been saying my prayers every night, and of course remembering you in them. I expect in my next letter I will have a lot more to say. I hope you are well. Yours lovingly, Zag.

I folded the thin pale blue airmail paper, and slotted my feeble letter into the envelope and sealed it. Oh, the bitter misery and humiliation of that hateful Sunday, and the cold loneliness of the last week. Tears of self-pity were, again, welling up futilely in my eyes. I could feel the burning, prickling sensation at the back of my eyelids.

I picked at the crumpled white sheets, and flung the envelope away from me crossly. Envelopes rarely fling well, and this one fluttered a few feet, then like a sickly butterfly glided quickly to the polished wooden floor. I lay back on to the warmly rumpled, fretful sheets and stared at the stark white ceiling.

I allowed the self-indulgent tears to continue to rise, brimming over my eyes and sliding forlornly down my face, to trickle, hot and wet, into my ears. I had been virtually ostracized since that loathsome Sunday, but what was worse, I didn't resent this rejection, but understood it and sympathized with it.

At the grim end of my graveside performance of vomiting, I had been too drained and weak to move. A circle of pairs of stunned, shocked eyes stared accusingly down at me. Even though I felt so ill, I sensed the mockery in Arabella's eyes and, in Ziggy's glittering stare, a concentrated loathing and mortification. To vomit so grossly and so vilely as soon as you set eye upon your father's grave was truly despicable, and even in my helpless muddle of weakness and nausea, I knew it.

From a million miles away, white starfish on long tentacles reached down from the dazzling blue sea of the sky, and then retreated; hands reaching down to pick me up and then withdrawing without touching me. I had managed to spray my stinking, hideous regurgitated breakfast not only over my father's headstone, but also amply over my clothes and body. Long straggles of hair were plastered sideways across my cheeks with a mixture of sweat and vomit. Dr Cairns, perhaps because of being a doctor, was prepared to sully his bony Scottish hands, but Mr Hannett held him back. Jacob, the assistant to the errant Father Mannering, was summoned to fetch a bucket of water.

He brought it over in a karai, a large handleless metal dish with a curved base. A silver, blinking moon hung and shimmered above me, and there was the sloshing softness of the sea on a harbour wall. Dr Cairns threw the water over me, and even as I gulped and blinked in its cool freshness, I noticed the faint sweet perfume of jasmine, rising above the stench of vomit. Mr Ballantine told me later that Jacob had scooped the water from the church's baptismal font, in which floated the dainty white blossoms of jasmine. I lay baptized at their feet, gasping helplessly like a stranded fish, in a pool of water and vomit. The water, as well as washing me, had soaked into the ever-thirsty earth, and the dry dust had become wet and glutinous. I felt sucked down into its red clay grip. I had rapidly become an object that was really too disgusting to be touched by the clean and sacred hands of white people.

Thus, the rest of the blurred, hazy Sunday was

91

washed in the liquid brown eyes of the native servants, their firm pink-palmed hands excavating me from the earth, lifting me, carrying me, and, back at Marsdon Villas, undressing me and washing me. They slid me into bed, and they held me and turned me, this way and that, as Dr Cairns and the paired gloating eyes of Richard and Andrew, his medical students, observed me and prodded me, both physically and with questions to which I didn't know the answers. All I wanted to do was sleep in the cool clean softness of the sheets, and try to block out and forget the accusing, despising, hard blue eyes of Ziggy that glittered hatefully at me from every drab recess of my mind.

When I had recovered sufficiently to know that I was achingly bored, two or three days later, I realized that I had been ostracized. Marsdon's parents and Arabella's parents would slink in and out of my room once, or even twice, each day, but they never stayed long and they always seemed uncomfortable.

The men would be heartily garrulous and falsely jovial, or so it seemed to me in my sad, critical and embittered mind, marching loudly around the wooden-floored room, their feet heavy and cumbersome. They would pick up objects and put them down again awkwardly, clatteringly, too large somehow for the room's detestable peachy femininity. Then they would clap their hands decisively, or slap their thighs, and stride quickly out of the room, for they had important things to see to. Their parting words were inevitably a humourless joke about their jealousy of my horizontal existence, lying in bed with nothing to do.

Lily and Mrs Hannett adopted a different approach. They would sit, perched delicately in cane chairs, on either side of my bed, and with soft, tinkling, breathy voices they would enquire again and again after each wretched part of my ugly body. They were probably only being kind, but my submerged impatience would finally break clear of my resignation, and I would snap crossly that I was fine, fine, fine. They would sigh then, as though it were they who were ill, and arch their eyebrows and pat their ageing hair.

'We're obviously tiring her, the poor dear,' they would silently mouth across my grumpy sickbed, and they would briefly rest their pale, warm hands or their dry, powdery lips on my cross, sweaty forehead, and then tiptoe daintily out of the room.

Apart from the brisk clinical daily visits by Dr Cairns, in which I had to squirm naked under his unamused, unforgiving, Scottish eye and the twitch of his ferocious moustache, nobody else came to visit me. I was pitifully grateful, however, when Max or Mr Hannett would gruffly mention that Mr Ballantine was asking after me, or had sent me his kind regards. I hugged these meaningless pleasantries tightly to myself, and wondered, with a helpless, torturing envy, how Arabella was progressing with her methodical capture of this young Scot in her honeyed web. I wondered if she had perceived the plaintive buzzing of the two foolish flies already snared, and I wished that one of them, Ziggy, would come and see me. He never did.

Boredom, therefore, drove me to start on Lily's literary offering. The only reading material in Marsdon Villas, apart from the bible, was Dickens. Marsdon had told me that there had once been a collection of superbly illustrated books about African wildlife, but he had taken them with him to school in England, and had not brought them back. His parents weren't interested in wildlife, apart from as pests or trophies. So, it was Dickens. A complete set, bound in opulent red leatheriness with their titles embossed in fanciful gold lettering on both the spines and fronts. The crisp freshness of their pages indicated that they had never been opened, let alone read.

Much as I loved to read, with that desperate greed for escape born in my restricted childhood, the grey, back-street worlds of Dickens took on the unreality of a half-remembered dream in Marsdon Villas. From my invalid position, propped on the tussle of pillows on my bed, all I could see through the open window was the mocking Kenyan sky. The sky was an unquestioning blue. I felt I could drink it, swim in it, drown in it. It went on for ever and for ever, and for always; the chill grey skies of a grimy London or desolate marshland did not exist. Or then it would rain, and the battering fury of the tropical downpour would amaze me. One of the servants would rush into my room, with barely a pause after knocking, and close the window; the insipid drizzle of Dickens was the whisper of a tedious shadow.

So I read little of *The Old Curiosity Shop* initially, but stared at the long rectangle of sky through the window, waiting for some company and fretting when I was honoured by a fleeting visit. I felt hideously sorry both for myself and for my inability, not only to be incapable of reaching through to Ziggy, but also to match up to his standards, impress his friends and to join his élite golden crowd.

Instead, peevish, hot, irritable and sad, I started to try and befriend the native servants. I knew that such a thing was 'not done', but out of a furious and perverse spitefulness, which I believe now was intended to be directed at myself rather than anyone else, I, without thinking, attempted this as a clumsy, rebellious gesture.

I clearly remember the first time that I really spoke to one of the native servants. Previously I had only managed to mumble 'yes, please' and 'no, thank you', and looked the other way in the foolish, shy manner of the unsure or those unaccustomed to being waited upon, of which I was both.

I had finished reading Chapter One of *The Old*

Curiosity Shop and was trying to interest myself in Chapter Two. I was not succeeding, however. I was hot, I was restless, I was thirsty and I was very bored. I flung the book crossly away from me (I closed it carefully first, however, for I didn't want to hurt its pristine pages, despite my irritation with it), and it thumped noisily on to the wooden floor. Despite being closed, it lay on the dark floorboards in a manner that seemed to describe, very obviously, that it had been fretfully discarded. The sun glinted on the gold of the embossed title letters, and by squinting at it I could see that it was winking at me like a malevolent red eye. I sighed; it would never do for Lily to find it there. I already felt that I was in a disguised form of disgrace, and I could perhaps be condemned to my solitary confinement in my room for even longer on the grounds of bad behaviour, which would also be disguised by some medical word – delirium or hysteria, perhaps.

As I swung my legs out of bed, my ugly wide-ankled legs struggling out from under the ruckled sheet shroud, one of the native servant women came into the room. I didn't think that she was the usual woman who looked after me, although I wasn't sure, but I was sure that she hadn't knocked on the door.

'You didn't knock.' My voice was loaded with imperious accusation.

'No. Sorry, Miss Zag. I thought I heard you knocking for me. Should you be getting out of bed?' She was looking at me directly, which was unusual, but her voice was very soft and humble. I found it hard to guess the age of negroes, but I knew that she must be older than forty. Her hair was tied in a bright piece of orange material, and she seemed very large in all the wrong, unattractive ways. I felt humble too.

'No. I suppose not. I was hot. I dropped my book. Could you give it to me? Please. It's over there, on the floor.' The distance between the bed and the book

95

belied the word 'dropped', but she picked it up and brought it to me without a flicker of change in her expression. I thrust my legs crossly back down into the bed.

'Thank you.' I paused, just for that brief, breath-gasping second, that made me aware that I was about to verge on to the trembling edge of permissible behaviour.

'I threw it, of course. I didn't drop it. It's a very dull book, and it's so hot and boring in here.' She smiled at me, or rather crinkled her eyes slightly, but didn't reply. Instead she looked down at her bulging belly, dropping her eyes respectfully. She was providing me with the opportunity to retreat. I blundered on.

'It is so lonely up here. Do you know what the others are doing? Marsdon, I mean, and Ziggy, my brother, and the Hannetts?' The words tumbled out of my nervous lips so guiltily fast that I wondered if she could have caught them. In retrospect, she probably didn't, for her English was not so good, and she only replied,

'No, Miss Zag,' without looking up at me.

'Perhaps you could stay and talk to me for a bit? Please. If you haven't anything else to do, of course.'

She didn't answer, but she raised her eyes to look at me, and she smiled. It was a tentative smile, but it was welcoming and broad in her round creased face. It revealed a mixture of brightly white teeth and grim grey-brown pointed stumps. She stood very formally in front of me, her hands clasped before her. Despite the gentle friendliness in her plump face and the warmth of her ragged smile, I felt she was waiting for orders.

'Please sit down, won't you?' I pointed with the back of my hand at one of the delicate cane chairs with peach cushions that either Lily or Mrs Hannett usually perched neatly upon. For a second I had a horrifying mental image of this large native servant woman either breaking the chair, or worse still, getting stuck in it. Her backside seemed to be the widest part of her huge round figure.

'No thank you, Miss Zag, I'd rather stand. If you do not mind.' Her English seemed strangely blurred to me, totally comprehensible, but somehow peculiarly different. I had a vague image of the book of Impressionist paintings I'd pored over in the library in Cornwall with Marsdon.

'Well. What's your name?'

'Florence, Miss Zag.'

'Just Florence? Nothing else?'

'Oh no. I have many other names, but that's the only one you will understand. The others are very . . .' she paused and then, carefully, '. . . primitive.'

'Oh?'

'Everyone who works in Marsdon Villas is only allowed to use their English name; Christian name.'

'Oh?'

She smiled at me again, but remained silent.

'Where is . . . well, I don't know her name . . . the servant, the girl, who usually looks after me?'

'Beatrice is unwell today, Miss Zag.'

'Oh dear. I didn't know. What's wrong with her? I hope she isn't very ill.'

'No, no. Just the fever. The malair, Miss Zag.'

'Malaria. But that is bad.' No answer, just a slow smiling rolling of the head. Her eyes were twinkling. Then,

'For you, it is bad. For us it is not so bad. We're used to it and we are very strong.' She showed me her arms. They looked warm and buttery and, as she said, strong.

'I'll leave you now, Miss Zag,' and she moved towards the door. Despite her curious ungainly shape, she seemed to move very softly and elegantly, gliding rather than walking, with her back straight.

'No. Wait a second. Please. Florence.' She paused at

97

once, turning towards me and smiling. She seemed very serene, as though she were controlling the conversation, rather than I. Never really used to being the master of a situation, that seemed comforting to me, and I smiled too.

'So, when Beatrice is here, where do you work?'

'In the kitchen, Miss Zag. I prepare the vegetables mostly.'

'Please may I come and see you there, then? When I'm allowed to get up, I mean.'

'Of course, Miss Zag.' But her eyes looked grave and a little doubtful.

'I will then. Thank you.' She smiled at me again, gently but still doubtful. As I slouched back into the feathery squidge of pillows she slid, or rather sailed, like a billowy schooner cutting effortlessly and gracefully through the waves, out of my room.

Looking up at the blank whiteness of the ceiling I could smell again the warm, cheery, steamy, cosy comfort of Mrs O'Cavanagh's kitchen in Stoney Street, and I could hear echoing, somewhere in the memories clustered in disorder in my brain, Max's jovial rumble to the gentle clink of tea cups, '. . . please do feel free to go into the kitchen any time you like . . .'

Florence brought me my dinner that evening, carried smoothly on a tray in her strong arms. Mrs Hannett came with her 'just to check that you're eating properly and not picking'. I tried to give Florence a conspiratorial smile, but her eyes were averted, looking always deferentially downwards. It was as though we had never met.

The following day, Beatrice was back. I suppose that I'd never really noticed her previously. She was just one of the native women who worked in Marsdon Villas. Unlike the houseboys in their stiff white uniform, almost naval in appearance with braid and shining buttons, the women dressed in an amorphous selection

98

of flowered frocks and their hair was wrapped in bright squares of cloth. Perhaps I give the impression that Marsdon Villas was swarming with an army of toiling house servants, and initially, I suppose, it did seem that way to me. There was invariably an anxiously polite and immediately obedient black assistant on hand when anything was needed, and very often they seemed to anticipate what was going to be needed. However, as I started to take notice of them, I recognized individuals amongst the troops of dutiful, complaisant minions, and my first wild estimate of hundreds shrank to no more than a dozen, including the couple of gardeners.

I looked with interest at Beatrice as she brought in my breakfast, and placed it carefully on the white-painted wood and wicker table next to my bed; the usual slice of succulent pawpaw and mug of steaming coffee. She was much younger than Florence and slimmer too, but I could see that, like Florence, her bare upper arm showed that rich buttery wobble that implied strength. As Beatrice pulled open the peach-white curtains and opened the windows to the glistening blue of the morning, I looked cautiously at my own pallid upper arm. It reminded me, unpleasantly, of the freshly plucked woodcock that Aunt Bernice sometimes prepared for Sunday lunch in Cornwall: decidedly scrawny and weak.

'Florence said you were ill.' She turned back from the window quickly. She was startled. She stared at me with her big eyes, and then lowered them quickly, embarrassed and a little scared. I was also startled. I hadn't been sure I would be bold enough to continue this chatting with the native servants, and the sentence had spurted out of my lips in a way that surprised me too.

'Yes, Miss. I was yesterday. I'm sorry.' This was perhaps the first time I'd felt the pleaure of power over anyone, but it was a flickering, quickly passing feeling.

'I hope it wasn't anything you'd caught from me. Florence thought it was malaria. Are you sure you shouldn't be in bed today?' A quick flash of a smile, a dart of purple-pink gums and glinting white teeth,

'Oh yes. I'm much better today, Miss Zag.' I noticed that, to my surprise, Beatrice was a lighter, glossier, more golden shade of brown than Florence. I had really not observed these people at all before, just colouring them with my unseeing eyes, a uniform coat of matt black. I wondered if shade was determined by inheritance or exposure to the sun or age or what.

'How old are you, Beatrice?'

'Twenty-one, Miss Zag.'

'I am sixteen.'

'Yes, Miss Zag.' She was looking nervously at the door now from under her lowered lids, unsure of whether to go, and possibly offend me, or stay, and perhaps offend her employers. She knew, as I knew, that my talking to the servants like this, despite its stilted formality, was not a thing that would be fostered within Marsdon Villas.

'I'm sorry if you don't like to talk to me. It's my fault. I'm very lonely here. I told Florence that I would go and visit her in the kitchen. When I'm allowed to get up, that is.'

Silence. Just a shy darting smile and a blinking glint from her brown eyes. I felt frustrated. I felt that what I now perceived as my bold and rebellious efforts to nibble away at the foundations of the superior white grouping of Marsdon Villas, that had both ostracized me and belittled the natives, were not receiving the support and encouragement that they should. I picked up my coffee mug and slurped at its hot steamy bitter sweetness, looking down into it at my eyes reflected in the black shining surface. Beatrice, moving with that gliding straight-backed grace that I had seen in Florence, slid silently out of the room. The door clicked closed behind her and tears of querulous self-indulgence welled, brimmed and rolled down my face into the coffee, breaking up my reflected eyes into a million shining splinters.

'I only wanted to be friends,' I muttered petulantly, putting down the coffee mug and leaning back, but there was nobody there to hear. I looked up at the unresponsive white ceiling and out to the rectangle of indifferent blue sky streaked with the faintest white whisper of a high-up cloud. I could feel the complacent bitterness of the martyrdom of being an outcast curling and writhing deep inside me. I had failed in Cornwall, I had failed in Marsdon Villas, most of all I had failed in Ziggy.

The loneliness of my bedridden Marsdon Villas existence continued. I continued reading Dickens and I continued talking to the servants who came into my room during the course of their various duties. Eventually Dr Cairns said that I could be allowed to get up; I had been in bed two weeks and it seemed like two centuries. However, surprising progress had been made. I had completed *The Old Curiosity Shop* and was halfway through *Great Expectations*, but more surprisingly I was also on friendly terms, in a secret, stilted, formal way, with half of the native servants. The white occupants of Marsdon Villas seemed more remote from me than ever before.

Chapter Eight

Marsdon Villas, Kericho, Kenya.
Dear Aunt Bernice,

This is my third letter to you from Marsdon Villas, so we must have been here almost six weeks. In some ways it seems like much longer – not because it is dull or boring, but because I am getting accustomed to the relaxed way of living, and the beautiful weather is no longer a surprise to me. I have completely recovered from my mystery illness that I was suffering from in my last letter, although when I was allowed out of bed I was initially quite weak.

Max, Lily, Marsdon, Ziggy and Arabella have been away for ten days near a town called Nanyuki which if you look on the atlas you might see is very near the foot of Mount Kenya. Max had some business or something to do there with some white people who have a farm there, and the others went along for the trip. I would have liked to have gone too, but Dr Cairns thought that so soon after my illness it might have been unwise. I am sorry that I wasn't allowed to go, but I am sure Dr Cairns was very sensible in making that decision, and now I am looking forward to hearing all about it when they get back. Did you know that Mount Kenya is the second highest mountain in Africa (Kilimanjaro is higher)? As we are here for such a long time I am sure I will be allowed to accompany everyone on any other trips which are made.

Of course I am enjoying just staying at Marsdon Villas anyway, so I am not complaining, and, of course, I am not alone here. Mr and Mrs Hannett are staying here *still, although Mr Hannett is very busy and frequently has to travel to Nairobi to see people. He says it is such a relief to get back to Marsdon Villas after a day in the capital. Unfortunately, Mrs Hannett is not that well presently. Dr Cairns calls in nearly every day, and he says that it is stress. Certainly she is very nervous. Mr Ballantine says that she is worried that the blacks really will gain independence, and when Mr Hannett brings back any news of such an idea from the capital from such people as Mr Frobisher, then she gets very upset.*

I understand that just after Father came here in the 1940s there was some band of negro terrorists called the Mau Mau trying to bring about independence from us by violence. It sounds terrible. Mr Ballantine wasn't here then, but of course Max was and so were the Hannetts. Mrs Hannett went back to England and all the white men had to be in a sort of army against the terrorists, so that was Max and Mr Hannett too. That's over now and all the terrorists were killed or captured, but still it seems there is a high probability of independence. That is why the Hannetts are living at Marsdon Villas; Mrs Hannett doesn't want to have a house here because she is hoping to go to South Africa if independence looks imminent. I hope I've got all that right – you know how stupid at politics I am, and I never really listen when the men discuss these things. I have not seen the black servants at Marsdon Villas do anything other than be helpful and friendly, however, so I don't think that Mrs Hannett should worry too much.

I have not just been seeing the Hannetts. Mr Ballantine has taken me around the estate a little which has been very nice, and I have been to dinner at his house a few times with Dr Cairns and his two medical students, Richard and Andrew. Mrs Hannett doesn't like to be out of Marsdon Villas after dark, so the Hannetts don't come too.

As you can see, I have so many exciting things to do here, but I am still thinking of you and remembering you in my prayers each night. I hope that you are well and that it is not too stormy and wet in Cornwall. Yours lovingly, Zag.

Another pale blue airmail letter to be sent back to the dim Cornish mistiness, swollen with its plethora of sickly sweet semi-truths, and the address written carefully on the envelope. I stuck down the flap and carried the letter downstairs with me. I propped it neatly against the brass vase on the small wooden table, glowing dully with polish, in the hall. It would be taken to the post office in Kericho town on the next trip.

Teatime was over more than an hour ago, but the bright paint-blue of the afternoon still hung heavily across the garden. In less than two hours it would be dark. I wandered through the house to the back quarters and into the kitchen. With Ziggy, Arabella, Marsdon and his parents away and Mr Ballantine and Mr Hannett so busy with the tea plantation and Dr Cairns and his students so busy with their parasites and other medical problems, the kitchen had become my refuge from my own jealous boredom and from the tiresome fretfulness of Mrs Hannett.

The kitchen was a large room and satisfyingly square. It had two doors, one into the garden and one into the rest of the house. It was through the latter door that I invariably entered. Coolly stone-flagged and clean, there was always the pungent tang of the crunchy leafy spice of fresh coriander, or, in the morning, the burnt crispy caramel of freshly ground coffee.

Initially the servants had treated me with a frightened obsequiousness to pacify and repel an intruder, but perhaps my own pitiful timidity had been important in changing that. Instead, now, there was an almost schizophrenic relationship growing unacknowledged between us. In the kitchen the attitude of them to me was an amicable blend of courteous tact and jovial friendliness; outside the kitchen, the usual humble deference of the black servant towards the superior white skin still prevailed. I like to think, now, that this duplicity and double perspective suited the servants as agreeably as it fitted in with my life. If the Hannetts had realized that a familiarity was germinating behind the metaphorical green baize door (the door was wooden and painted white), they would have suffocated it quickly and harshly in its infancy. Perhaps the servants were merely playing a part to satisfy the whims of this awkward, odd, ugly white teenage waif, but even if this was so, the gratitude that I feel for that performance of welcoming warmth and pleased companionship is but only slightly diminished.

Florence and Beatrice were my favoured companions. I would sidle, shyly and quietly, into the kitchen, and just for a few brief seconds absorb its atmosphere, so different from that of the rest of the house: the pervasive aroma of coriander and coffee, overlaid with the scent of whatever was in preparation, the metallic slop and splash of water in the karais, and the sure regularity of chopping.

Samwel, the cook, would be peering forward into the steaming pots on the stove, his fine old mazed face wrinkled into permanent lines of anxiety that could so easily switch to hilarity. Perhaps two or three of the white-uniformed houseboys would be lolling indolently near him, propped against the white-washed walls and chatting in a slow, rolling tongue that I could not understand, but by the nudging of their relaxed elbows I knew that they would be talking about Samwel's cooking, and often gently teasing him about his culinary merit. Frequently the door to the garden would be pushed wide open and sometimes the houseboys would be standing in the doorway, warming their feet on the bouncing shafts of sunlight on the flagstones, and chewing on the green fibrous stems of some plant, unknown and exotic to me, and therefore nameless. Florence and Beatrice would be always busy, either chopping meat or vegetables with a certain, steady rhythm, or washing crockery, elbow-deep in slimed grey water. Their voices would be rolling musically onwards too, either talking to each other or chiming into the conversation of the houseboys.

Barely had I absorbed this regulated scene that I loved and wanted so much to be part of, than they would see me standing shy and uncertain in the doorway. Florence or Beatrice would call me in with the 'Karibu, karibu' of Swahili welcoming, and the houseboys would touch their foreheads in a friendly tease. The oldest one, a man of at least fifty, with his hair grey and his face knowing and thin, would pull up a four-legged rush-topped stool for me to sit upon demurely, embarrassed and yet somehow very pleased.

Samwel would show me what we were having for dinner, but his English seemed to be hazily tumbled in his memory and our communication was mostly limited to nods and smiles. I loved to watch the way he wiped away the spherules of sweat dancing out on his shining black forehead amongst the creases and wrinkles, for it was always too hot near the stove. He was very precise with his clean white cloth, and as he lowered it, the anxiety lines would tremble into a gap-toothed grin.

Florence and Beatrice, however, had apparently decided that I was their responsibility. Although I was happy just to sit idly and watch them, their backs bent and their strong arms and fingers moving knowingly and easily through their work, they would nearly always talk to me. They slid from their easy tribal language, that to me, because it was foreign and different from the prim ice of my own language, seemed beautiful and melodic, into a slightly mutilated English. I could never decide what was wrong with their English, but I knew that their phraseology was somehow outdated and almost biblical, and that the tenses were confused. I am pleased that I never corrected them, as I heard Lily, and more often Mrs Hannett, do, but I know that I subconsciously felt ridiculously and shamefully smug in my unilingual isolation, that I could speak a more correct version of my own language than they.

Florence seemed to try to mother me and shelter me, and I warmed to her as I had warmed to Mrs O'Cavanagh. Her patient smiling tolerance and her mountainous black figure of sunny amiability brought out feelings of a close, tender security inside me. I wanted to be gathered up in those huge, strong, buttery arms, snuggled into the harbour of the enormous bosom and feel eternally protected. Of course, these feelings remained stifled inside me, unacknowledged even by myself, and instead we smiled at each other across the yawning acres of cool flagstone floor. The shafts of sunshine dancing through the open doorway into the garden, alive with motes of dust, separated us like barricades of swords.

Beatrice was younger than Florence, and although she was married with two children her age made her closer to me in some ways. She was curious about me with a live, eager interest that made her reach out and touch my pale skin gently with one shyly extended forefinger, or pat my lank, wispy, mousy-blonde hair with the lightest touch of the pinkish palms of her black hands. She wanted to know about England and my home, and the whole kitchen would pause and listen to me as I answered her questions.

They would gasp and shake their heads in disbelief as I talked about the November weather that would be presently cutting its chill gloomy way into Britain's gusty streets and soggy fields, or nod wisely and mutter 'Mombasa' or 'Malindi' as I spoke with enthusiasm of the distant, dancing blue of the Cornish sea. I made small mention of my family, skirting Beatrice's question with a skill born of my schooldays of tortured teasing, and the shame of my father's grave was still etched deeply and branded into me. However, when I could not avoid mentioning my father or my mother's pitiful state, a gentle sigh of understanding and compassion would murmur in ripples through the kitchen.

It seemed so strange to me, but in many ways I felt that this group of listening black people, perhaps six or seven of them, a mix of ages, sexes and experiences, but all Kenyan negroes, understood me better than anybody else I had ever met. This thought would come and grasp my mind at unpredictable times, not when I was seated in the kitchen, but sometimes when I was cleaning my teeth at night, wandering with Mr Ballantine along the dirt tracks between the fields of warm green tea and, most frequently, as Mrs Hannett cluttered peevishly to Mr Hannett about the incorrigible ignorance and brazen stupidity of blacks over a piqued and rankled dinner or breakfast. The thought would steal up in my mind unbidden and it possessed me with a sense of hopeless foreboding, loneliness and dread. It made me long for my golden brother, my deific, wonderful Ziggy to come back, to hold and hug and understand me. I knew these longings were hopeless, foolish and despicable.

Despite my anguished jealousy at being deprived of joining the trip to Nanyuki, one thing which cheered and pleased me in my selfish and narrow way was the enforced separation of Arabella Hannett and Tom Ballantine. I noted that he continued to call at Marsdon Villas with a frequent regularity despite Arabella's absence, and that these calls were not always to discuss the state of the tea with Mr Hannett, but were also social visits for the ritual of afternoon tea in the garden beyond the veranda.

Although I realized that these visits were not intended to be for my benefit and entertainment, but more polite calls of perceived duty, I was always excited and flustered when I heard his cheery Edinburgh accent calling out and heard the crunch of the Marsdon Villas gravel drive under his confident stride. I would be embarrassed and silent as we sipped our tea in the hot green-blue of the afternoon, my hands both sticky and slippery with an unbidden sweatiness. Unable to slip into the easy indulgences of inane and civilized chatter, I would toy with the sugar bowl, heaping the white crystals into sliding mountains, and inwardly brood on the horror and humiliation of my father's grave.

Mr Ballantine seemed unaware of, or at least unperturbed by my gangling social awkwardness and uncomfortable ineptness, and despite it, he would gravely invite me to his small dinners in his long white bungalow. I would accept with my inevitable gauche clumsiness, trying not to appear too eager.

At his dinners I could relax a little. Although Richard and Andrew could easily make me feel intellectually inferior, socially they appeared as bungling and foolish as I, and Dr Cairns, with his gruff Glasgow formality, seemed to intimidate us all equally. Often these dinners would lapse into almost silent affairs, the banal and meaningless small talk having been exhausted within the first half-hour. I was content to sit in the soft quiet of the Kenyan dark and drink in the gentle sweet scent of jasmine and tobacco, and the huge luminosity of the African night sky, flittered with the leathery wings of the bats that roosted in the eaves of Mr Ballantine's bungalow and with the low, green-white blinking stars of fireflies.

The native woman that Mr Ballantine employed

109

would serve the meal, sliding silently and coolly behind us in her bare feet. He would speak to her in the language that only I could not understand, but I could hear, from so much uncomprehending listening, the ripples of happy laughter in her quiet replies of only a few words. The male servant would sit outside on the veranda, a shadow blacker even than the darkness, smoking and silently watching the deep engulfing chasm of the night. When she had served us, the woman would join him and from where we sat at the quiet dinner table we could vaguely hear the murmuring cadences of their conversation. Both the servants were young, the man perhaps twenty-three, and the woman, slim and elegantly beautiful, barely twenty. I suppose I assumed they were married, or anyway in love, and I imagined a dreamy romance in their placid serenity on the night-time veranda which often made me feel the forlorn, jabbing sorrow of a wistful envy.

In spite of these pangs of melancholy jealousy, the peaceful tranquillity of these evenings and dinners in Mr Ballantine's home brought a sort of happiness with them. Sometimes I would steal a shy smile towards Mr Ballantine, trying to express some sort of gratitude, and, perhaps, longing. He would meet my smile across the polished dark wood of the table with those blue, tired eyes with the oriental slant, and his large mouth would iron his lines of tiredness into an answering smile. I might try to read a hidden message in this return smile, but I knew it was a foolish delusion. Dr Cairns or Richard or Andrew might smile at me likewise across the gleaming table top, but to me their expressions were devoid of the meaning I sought for with Mr Ballantine.

The Sunday after I had written my third letter to Aunt Bernice, I returned to the church for the first time since my previous humiliating visit. There were only the seven of us in the congregation; the Hannetts, Dr

110

Cairns, Andrew, Richard, Mr Ballantine and I, and our singing sounded lost and thin in the fennelly coolness. The service was as tedious as before, and the prayers, which included one for the safe travel and return of 'our dear friends' rose haphazardly to the ceiling and stayed there. There was not enough love and force in the prayers to push them even into the vast blue of the sky; heaven was out of the question. The National Anthem struggled out slowly and flatly, and we scurried from the church in shame at our poor performance.

Father Mannering and Jacob nodded and blessed us at the door, but again it was as soulless and methodical as duties at a factory conveyor belt. I knew that there had been prayers for me when I was ill, for both Lily and Mrs Hannett had delighted in telling me about them as I lay in my angry, rumpled bed, but Father Mannering did not greet me back into his fold. I wondered if he had recognized me or even noticed me at all, and I rather doubted it.

Again it was gaspingly hot outside the church as compared to its cool interior, but this time we did not pause at my father's fated grave. I could see, by a covert sideways glance, that my iniquity had been cleansed away, and fresh clods of turf were stamped in around the stone and wooden cross.

On the red dusty road the three cars glittered like angry insects in the sun: the Hannetts', Dr Cairns' and Mr Ballantine's. I had driven to the church with the Hannetts and Andrew and Richard always travelled with their mentor, Dr Cairns. Mr Ballantine paused as he swung into his stifling car.

'Zag, why don't you ride back to Marsdon Villas with me?' I flushed. I could feel the mixture of shame and pride burning on my sweaty cheeks.

Mr Ballantine's car smelt of heat and leather and the sweet scent of drying tea leaves. His houseboy was driving and Mr Ballantine and I sat together in the back. Neither of us spoke, and we both looked out of our respective windows, closed against the billows of dry red dust and the children screaming and hooting and scampering and tumbling after us. Even as we were approaching the drive of Marsdon Villas neither of us had spoken, and I could feel my cheeks were still flushed, but the shame was mingled with disappointment now rather than pride.

'Zag,' and I could see that the worry lines were etched deeper on Mr Ballantine's forehead, 'Molly, my housegirl, and Albert's cousin,' he paused and nodded his head towards the driver of the car. The dark face remained impassive and I wondered if Albert understood English. 'She is the sister of the girl Beatrice that works in Marsdon Villas. Do you know Beatrice?' I nodded. I realized now how similar Beatrice and Molly appeared; both tall and with their skins a delicious toast and honey brown rather than black, and with a supple, lithe grace in their walk and actions.

'Molly tells me that you are spending a lot of time in the kitchen at Marsdon Villas, Zag. Believe me, although this may not seem right to you, it can be difficult if you become too close and friendly with the servants. Apart from blurring the line between master and servant, black people are, well, different to us. I am sure you realize that neither Marsdon's parents nor the Hannetts would encourage you to befriend the native servants, and in many ways they are right. They have lived in this country a lot longer than you, and a lot longer than me, and they know from experience the best way to treat the blacks. Father Mannering has had many problems because of his actions and beliefs, as I think Max has told you. Of course, we are all human, black and white, as Max so often says, but please do be circumspect. I'm not wanting to preach to you. I am just trying to warn you to be careful.'

All this was said in a flurry of words which although not garbled or rushed, but clear and gravely precise, seemed nevertheless to be hurried. As we crunched up the gravel drive to Marsdon Villas and stopped by the front door, he looked into my sly face with concern in his oriental blue eyes, but his words had confused and muddled me. It had been such a strange thing for him to say to me; I had expected an outright and open condemnation for my loiterings in the kitchen with the servants, tinged perhaps with ridicule and disgust. Instead he had issued me with a warning, delivered anxiously in the relative privacy of his car and with no indication that my sins were to be disclosed to anybody else. The fact that he knew of my behaviour from his own housegirl, Molly, implied that he had spoken to her, and I had observed friendly relations between Mr Ballantine and both Molly and Albert which belied his advice against talking to the servants.

I felt that if I could concentrate just a little harder on what he had said, some great mystery would be disclosed to me and I would understand, but it was too late. We were clambering out of the hot stuffy car and the other two cars were also emptying in front of Marsdon Villas, for everybody had been invited for Sunday lunch. Instead I smiled up at him and said, 'Thank you for the lift in your car, Tom,' and feeling puzzled and unhappy, for the first time went deliberately up to Andrew and Richard and asked them how their parasitological research was progressing.

Throughout the long, lethargic swelter of Sunday lunch and Sunday teatime and the heat of a Sunday afternoon that was perspiring towards Sunday dinner, neither Mr Ballantine nor I made any mention of our strangely punctuated, quiet drive back from the church. Neither did I call him Tom again, but addressed him with my usual pitiful respect as Mr Ballantine. The event had seemed like a heat-induced dream. As he and the Hannetts lolled in idle, tedious conversation about tea and politics, Andrew and

Richard regaled me with idle, tedious, faecal anecdotes as we wandered through an idle, tedious game of croquet.

Dr Cairns joined neither group, but sat in the shade by the jasmine reading through a pile of medical journals that had reached him the previous Friday, already one month out of date. His eyebrows were hunched in a frown of angry concentration and he flicked his red-haired hands at the pester of flies with a series of irritated jerks. I asked Richard and Andrew what they thought of Dr Cairns, for their parasite tales were beginning to cling about me like an ill-defined and unpleasant smell, but they seemed not to have ever considered the character and nature of their mentor and tutor. They viewed life down the eyepiece of a microscope and all they seemed to see was the regular, repeated shapes of helminth eggs in a smear of faecal debris and an angular scatter of crystals. All the time I tried to contemplate the dream-like and curious, cautionary advice that Mr Ballantine had given me, but his words rattled and clanged in my skull, and as they danced to an unknown, juddering time, their meaning became yet more of an impenetrable mystery.

In the dark softness of the early, empty night, as the Hannetts creaked and sighed into the anonymity of their bed, I tiptoed barefoot down into the kitchen. The staff had not yet all drifted back to the smoke and clutter of their homes, and the kitchen lights were always the last to fade in Marsdon Villas. Beatrice was finishing washing the dinner service, and Florence was selecting a pawpaw for our breakfast from a pile of the large greenish fruit streaked with the yellow-orange of sunset ripeness. The other staff had already left, but two men were slouched in the doorway to the garden. They were dressed in peaked caps and raggedy dark blue uniforms that smudged into the deepness of the garden night. They were the gardeners I had watched from my bedroom window so many sunlit days before.

114

'Miss Zag! You should be in your bed!' There was a tired chiding in Florence's voice. 'We are almost ready to leave for our beds too.'

'Mr Ballantine said . . . said Molly said . . . said Beatrice said . . .' a fading, muddled petulance, and then, 'I didn't know she was your sister.'

Beatrice smiled, a quick lilt of a smile, but she remained silent. Florence too did not say a word, but one of the men by the door laughed, a quick, short, almost angry laugh.

'There is a lot you do not know, little spy at the window.' His voice was full of mocking laughter, and he lazily rolled his head on the door jamb so that he was facing in my direction. The kitchen brightness flicked across his face like light dropping through the oily calm of deep harbour water at night.

'Onyango!' Florence's voice held warning and reproof. Then to me, more gently, she added, 'Zag, these two are working here at Marsdon Villas as gardeners. They are Onyango and Charles.' The way she pronounced Charles, dividing it into two separately dropped syllables, Char-les, seemed strange to me, but the name Onyango surprised me more.

'I thought . . . well, Onyango is not an English name that I have heard before.' Again, it was not Florence's kindly, warm, safe tones that answered me, but the ringing, argent laughter from the garden door and mocking words falling lazily, slowly, carelessly, into the kitchen cool.

'I have no English name, little spy at the window. We are both strangers at this house, you and me, but you are the colour of power. I am from the Lake, little spy, the Lake where Juok, the god of my ancestors lives, but you choose to call it after a dead English queen who has never seen it.

'We are proud of our names at the Lake, little spy at the window, as we are proud of our fat tilapia, our brains, our uncircumcised bodies, and I will not lose

115

my name, my name that my mother, favourite wife of my father, gave me in the long pained evening of my birth. I refuse to lose my name, little spy, to satisfy a power that rules by colour alone.'

How young I was, how naive, to leave aside all those words of silver, taunting laughter, and smack outwards at the sting of the perceived insult,

'I was NOT spying at the window.' There was the furious petulance of the misunderstood in my reply, but Onyango only laughed a light, easy ripple of moonlight laughter.

Florence and Beatrice were ready to leave now and they tutted and chided at Onyango, while Char-les looked silently outwards, away from the kitchen, into the soft, deep darkness.

'Back to bed!' whispered Florence to me across the cool width of the kitchen, as they faded out into the sweet scent of the night garden.

'Good night,' called Onyango, quietly closing the door on Marsdon Villas. 'I will come and visit you again, little spy at the window.'

Indeed, after that, Onyango did become a frequent, if brief, visitor at the kitchen. Sometimes he would be accompanied by the silent Char-les, but often he would just put his own impish grin around the sunlit door frame.

'*Jambo,* little spy at the window,' he would say, laughing at me with his wicked, mocking eyes. Then he would walk away into the blinking blue-white dazzle of the sun-filled garden, leaving only the taunting shadow of his silvery laughter echoing wickedly through the still, cool emptiness of the kitchen and the hot, muddled turmoil of my mind.

Occasionally Char-les and Onyango would work in the back garden near the house, and I would be able to watch them from my bedroom window. Stripped to the waist, their blue shirts straddled carelessly over the wild, reaching arms of the tropical luxuriance, they would lean and straighten and swing their bodies as they chopped or dug, with a rhythmic strength.

Onyango was much darker than Char-les, and his back, glistening with the sweat of physical effort, would gleam in the sun like a polished dark wood or trickling black silk. If he saw me watching he would straighten up and stare boldly back at me, perhaps giving a mock salute or twitching his cap by its sweat-shadowed edge. Within only a few days I realized that I was looking out for Onyango's wicked grin and taunting laugh with an eager anticipation, and if I did not see him I would feel a perturbing pit of emptiness inside me as I curled up alone in my bed at night.

Mr Ballantine's warnings had not gone unheeded in my mind, but throughout the long, burnished week with him and Mr Hannett poring over the tea accounts, Dr Cairns and his students out on their parasite hunts and medical trips and Mrs Hannett in an endless fretful doze in the drawing room or on the veranda, the kitchen was my only refuge of human sanity.

One afternoon Beatrice brought in her two children for me to meet. Godfrey, four years old and as serious and wise as an ancient scholar, with his huge, bulging eyes rimmed with long crinkling eyelashes that had in babyhood learned the valuelessness of tears, studied me with a silent, knowing stare. Humphrey was two years old and still a naked toddling baby, his body gleaming and folded into dark soft pleats of pliant baby flesh. They played together very quietly in a corner of the kitchen, cowering into the shadows at the looming prospect of my grotesquely smiling pale face and staring, wide-eyed, up at me.

I picked up Humphrey and held his round wriggling body close against me, breathing in the warm grassy scent of his short-cropped, tickling hair and the oily, supple folds of his neck. The gurry odours of his doubtless wormy bottom, that would so interest Andrew and Richard, also whispered up to me, but rather than revolting me I felt unfamiliar upwellings of tenderness. Humphrey, however, was frightened in the grip of these strange, scrawny, pallid arms and squirmed free without uttering a cry. I kissed the rough stubble of his head as his baby-chub legs reached down to the stone floor of the kitchen, and Florence and Beatrice shouted and clapped their capable hands with delight.

Beatrice was pregnant again. If the child was a boy he would be called Geoffrey, to join the rhythm of Humphrey and Godfrey, but if the child was a girl . . . It is flattering for a mother to wish to give her unborn child your name, but if your name is Zag, perhaps the issue is an ethical and moral one too. I nodded and beamed with pleasure; I would be delighted to have a child named after me. It was a feeble clutch at immortality, I suppose, and the hope of a different and possibly more rewarding life.

Onyango flickered into the room with his light, easy step.

'The little spy at the window is corrupting our children already, I see. You must teach them to bow to you now, for they will be adults when our country is no longer run from your tiny, distant, freezing island. Now, don't look cross, little spy at the window, I have no children for you to taint, so I don't mind. I know that you are really a new colonial anyway, despising the past and afraid of the future.' Onyango's eyes were dancing with splintered shards of laughter that belied the potential seriousness in his words.

He walked further into the kitchen and then bent down to Humphrey to pick him up, swinging him high into the air in his strong arms with a loving affection that seemed to me an unusual thing for a man to show. He held Humphrey against his shoulder and the child poked his small dirty fingers into Onyango's wide-lipped mouth, tapping his broken black-edged fingernails against Onyango's teeth. Onyango held the little pestering hand away.

'Of course, even after independence is reached, I fear that your breed of new colonials, and even the old ones, will flourish for a long time. We will be ruled from behind, instead of from in front.'

He put the child down on the floor with wide-eyed, serious Godfrey and strolled back towards the garden door. He paused on the threshold and turned to me with his broadest, wickedest grin of triumph. 'After all, Jacob will always be known as Father Mannering's catamite, never the other way around, and that is due to colour as well as age.' Another quick flash of the pink wet gums and the white teeth and he had gone. I wondered if there was a dictionary in Marsdon Villas and wondered how Onyango, unlike the other natives, had managed to acquire an English that was not only fluid and precise, but had a vocabulary that vastly outshone my own.

It was Sunday again, and there had been no rain all week. The world seemed hot and tired and very dusty, and I felt hot and tired and faded. In the cool of the church I looked again at the dull, forgettable face of Father Mannering and the dark, doe-like, luminous eyes of Jacob, and murmured gently to myself 'catamite, catamite'. There was no dictionary at Marsdon Villas.

I wondered if I could dare to ask Dr Cairns, who sat beside me on the wooden pew, for a definition. I knew, however, that the angry bristling of his sandy moustache intimidated me too much and instead I resolved to ask Mr Ballantine, if he should suggest I travel back to Marsdon Villas in his car as on the previous Sunday. He did not, however, and I rode in ignorance back up the red scorched dusty track with the Hannetts.

It was too hot for croquet after lunch. Mrs Hannett

went to a darkened room with a glass of iced lemonade and a petulant headache, and Dr Cairns slept under a medical paper on a wicker chair in the shade of the veranda with his long legs stretched out in front of him. Mr Ballantine and Mr Hannett sat a little away from him, but also in the shade of the veranda. They were discussing the tea crop again in low, serious murmurs. Mr Ballantine's face was more lined and worried than ever, his blue slanted eyes buried deep down in pouches of swollen tiredness. The continuing dryness of the weather was causing him a sleepless concern and Max was not due back for two days. He fidgeted restlessly in his chair, frequently glancing up at the cruel endless blue of the sky as if trying to will rain clouds into existence.

If there had been no other company I would have gratefully retreated into the haven of the kitchen and whiled away the torpor and sweaty lethargy of the afternoon talking to Florence and Beatrice. They were also hoping for rain, and Samwel said that he scented it in the hot, rancid air

He had stood, still and silent, in the kitchen doorway the previous evening, his eyes screwed closed and his wide flare-nostril nose twitching delicately at the dry night heat. We, Beatrice, Florence and I, had held ourselves motionless and tense, watching Samwel in his strangely lagomorphic and concentrated posture at the door. Then he had turned, and smiled his deep, wrinkled, wise smile and we had relaxed and breathed again.

'Rain before end of week.' He seemed pleased and Beatrice and Florence showed complete confidence in his prediction. I expressed no doubts, but the unquestioning faith that Beatrice and Florence had in Samwel's calmly uttered words perturbed me. I knew I could not match this uncritical belief.

Now Richard and Andrew were also here with their probing intelligent eyes and sharp pigeon noses.

Richard had acquired a minor gut infection, so Andrew informed me with an undisguised malice and delight, that gave him mild stomach cramps and a vicious, rumbling flatulence. Richard looked uncomfortable, almost vulnerable, as Andrew gloated over his problems. He rolled his mouth around Richard's symptoms as though tasting them at a gourmet banquet. I pitied Richard, for I empathized with his plight of revolting helplessness, but I was also dispassionately interested to recognize that this was the first time I had observed Richard and Andrew acting as separate individuals.

Usually they seemed more like a single unit than a pair, but now as Andrew teased, and luxuriated in his friend's discomfort and seemed almost to welcome the bursts of gasping, sulphurous farts, I realized with surprise that they even looked remarkably different. Richard was short and dark. He had tanned to a deep, syrupy coffee shade that made him almost Asiatic in appearance. Andrew, however, was taller with a mouldy-blond muddle of hair, and his fair skin had burnt and freckled and peeled, resulting in his face, particularly his nose, becoming a blotchy patchwork of tender pink and sawdust. I was amazed that I had not noticed these obvious physical dissimilarities before, especially as I secretly imagined myself as a coolly careful and accurate observer of people. Nevertheless, as Andrew gradually tired of teasing Richard, and they both resumed the same dull, earnest, medical-student image, they blurred and overlapped, and the two pairs of gooseberry eyes and the two pointed, questing beaks became confused and merged to one.

We started to stroll down the garden, away from the house and around it, leaving behind us the anxious veranda with its dubious and unspoken history. The dry grass crackled crossly beneath our feet, and I was reminded of the long ago, scorching, fissile summer in Cornwall when Ziggy had first introduced me to the concept of friends by bringing Arthur Dobson to stay. I wondered where Dobson would be now. I could picture him so clearly still, his short swarthy body bristling with coarse dark hair and the potential to sprout yet more. Even the two dark half-moons of sweat in the armpits of his short-sleeved shirt, that I'd first glimpsed as he'd jumped from the train after Ziggy, still held a position in my memory that was both fond and sad, but also hopelessly confused.

'Penny for your thoughts?' How I hated that trite expression. I winced, but I hope it was only an inward wince. It probably was, for I was good at them through long practice. Andrew and Richard were watching me eagerly with their bulging eyes full of curiosity. I supposed that I had been smiling.

'Oh. Nothing really. I was just remembering a very hot summer at home. Ziggy had brought a friend to stay and I was just thinking about him.' I watched the ugly eyes of Andrew and Richard meet across me and their eyebrows skip with little, knowing twitches. I felt angered and annoyed by their worldly superiority and innuendo. I also felt annoyed that I wished their thoughts really did have some basis in reality.

'Oh, come on you two. I hardly knew him. He was Ziggy's friend, not mine. He spent the whole time with Ziggy and I was very young anyway. It was ages and ages ago.'

Perhaps the heat was making me irritable, for there was a high, screeching note of peevishness in my words. We were at the bottom of the garden now, walking along the perimeter fence by the dirt track, and my petulant whine seemed to raise red dust eddies on the track on the other side of the fence. Just as I clipped my mouth shut on my words, Onyango and Char-les were directly in front of us, no more than ten feet away.

They were squatting side by side on the withered dry grass with their sharp-edged machetes glinting brightly beside them. They were stripped to the waist as usual and their backs shone with perspiration. Their caps were pushed back on their heads and I could see drops of sweat glistening on their temples and broad noses too. They stood up quickly when they saw us and Char-les bobbed and nodded deferentially, looking down at his bare feet splayed amongst the yellow spikes of grass. Onyango touched his cap in his typical, familiar manner. I knew that he was mocking us by the skips of laughter in his merry eyes that stared straight at me, although his face stayed serious and even courteous.

'Miss Zag! I thought that I heard your oh-so-dulcet voice just now. I see that you are strolling. Beatrice mentioned to me that you were looking for a dictionary yesterday. You will not find one here. However, I can guess perhaps the definition that you were searching for. It is spelt with a C. Perhaps these two able and gifted young men could help you.'

I flushed furiously. Onyango was not playing the dual role that all the other native servants had so easily adopted, but was brazenly displaying his familiarity with me. How dare he try to embarrass me in this manner! I felt the vicious rage of humiliation bubbling uncontrollably inside me. I was too infuriated to analyse any feelings then however, and I swung past without acknowledging either him or Char-les. Andrew and Richard were looking at me with an unsuppressed and fascinated curiosity which made their previous expressions of interest in my thoughts of Dobson fade into benign insignificance.

'Do you know him?' they chorused before we were even out of earshot. Their voices held identical inflections of amazed disbelief and horrified astonishment.

'No!' I spat out the answer with a vehemence and fury that I did not know that I possessed. 'I believe that he is employed here. He should be working now. They were obviously shirking their duties at the bottom of the garden. Laziness is something that, quite rightly, neither Max nor Lily can abide. Tell them to get back to work, will you?'

I stalked angrily onwards and up towards the veranda without pausing or looking back. Andrew or Richard, or more probably both of them, strode back to where Onyango and Char-les stood. I could hear the imperious, hateful shout, 'Why aren't you working, you lazy oafs. Get to work or you'll lose your jobs.'

The words were rumbling and echoing through my brain as I walked into the house past the still-sleeping Dr Cairns, and Mr Ballantine and Mr Hannett in their earnest conversation. I did not go to the kitchen, but straight to my room where I flung myself sideways across the bed, pressing my face into the cool smoothness of the sheets. I was hot and flushed with the shame and hypocrisy of my actions and I knew that the scalding tears that coursed down my cheeks would not be enough to wash away the stains of my empty, stupid pride or blot out the words, my words and the medical students' words that thundered round and round my head, crashing off my skull and bludgeoning my mind into a state of wretched repentance and the desperate hope that I would be forgiven.

Dinner seemed a silent, awkward affair that night with yawning, screaming gaps between the pattering snatches of inane conversation. Probably it was no more awkward or silent than usual, but to me, every moment under the dark, watchful eyes of the houseboys that served the meal seemed laden with accusation and recrimination. I picked at my food without enthusiasm and I knew I was becoming a sour reflection of Mrs Hannett, sitting across the table from me and likewise toying with her cutlery. By the time we scratched back our chairs and left the debris of the meal for the servants to clear, I had a resounding, crunching headache. With muttered, downward-staring apologies

124

I scuttered off to my bed before Mr Ballantine and Dr Cairns and his students had left.

I lay in my hot, heavy bed and stared upwards at the ceiling. I had never felt more angrily wide awake. I listened to the noises around the house and tried to lose myself in the distant rattle and clatter of its existence. There was the dinner table being cleared; the scrape of metal on china and the clash of the silver cutlery being piled together. There was the meaningless ritual of good nights as Dr Cairns left with Andrew and Richard, and the cough, rattle and crunch of them driving down the drive and on to the track. The roar of the car engine was quickly engulfed by the silent solidity of the night. Mr Ballantine left shortly afterwards; I could hear a low murmur of conversation in the hallway and then Mr Ballantine's cheery 'G'night' followed by a smart, loud slam of the front door. Again the noise of his departing car was all too quickly submerged into the surrounding blackness. I could hear these sounds of life so clearly, but they seemed secondary. Above them rolled relentlessly an angry, aching hum of accusation reverberating through my head.

The Hannetts went to bed early too, soon after Mr Ballantine had left. I could hear the plaintive, whispered creaks of them settling down into sleep. Mr Hannett had a business meeting in Nairobi the following afternoon and would have to leave Marsdon Villas soon after breakfast. After some discussion he had agreed to take Mrs Hannett with him.

She was becoming desperate for the relaxation of some more white European company and the imminent return of Max, Lily and the others was not soon enough. She needed the sympathy and empathy of some other querulous wives and she knew she could find this in the capital. The black skins that surrounded Marsdon Villas were, so she said, suffocating her. Her obvious, frantic anguish when Mr Hannett seemed uncertain as to whether she could accompany him on his trip to Nairobi had resulted in Dr Cairns intervening in his hard, guttural, unforgiving Glaswegian accent. He clearly was hoping that a trip to Nairobi might reduce the series of neurotic ailments that Mrs Hannett was confronting him with on an almost daily basis. Mr Hannett had relented and they had arranged to have dinner with the Frobishers and to stay the night with them also.

I wished that I had asked if I too could accompany them, for although they had not offered this, they would have found it difficult to refuse. Like Mrs Hannett I was beginning to feel swamped and isolated in the world of Marsdon Villas. I felt like a trapped stranger in a foreign and dangerous country in which the complicated laws had never been explained to me. Nevertheless, I knew I would have been equally uncomfortable in the peevish and unwelcoming company of the Hannetts and it would only be one day and one night until not only they returned, but also Max, Lily, Marsdon, Arabella, and more importantly, Ziggy.

The Hannetts' bedroom sighed into the quiet breaths of sleep and, without thinking, I was out of bed and running barefoot down the cool stairwell towards the back of the house. By the kitchen door I paused, not to gather my thoughts or to contemplate my actions, but to catch my breath. Then I flung open the door and went in. This was not my normal timid, hesitant entry, but a desperate, impetuous bursting in which left me standing in the middle of the kitchen before I had even noticed who was in the room.

'Who is this? Surely I don't know this creature, this colonial, superior, little spy at the window?'

Onyango and Char-les slouched nonchalantly at the kitchen door. Beatrice was briskly putting away the dinner-time cutlery and Florence was standing watching her. The faces of the latter three were both blank and cautious, with their thoughts concealed behind neutral expressions. Contempt and hostility were

126

painted in bold clear sweeps across not only Onyango's face but every leaning inch of his black body. His voice was ringing with loathing, arrogance and derision. I gasped. I could feel my chest, perhaps my lungs, gathering in pain, and then it was out.

'I'm sorry, I'm sorry, I'm sorry, I'm sorry.' My face was suddenly buried in Florence's massive chest and my sobs, huge, gulping, snorting, rearing sobs, tore out of me as though they would never stop. Florence's big warm arms came heavily around my narrow heaving shoulders and pressed me into the bulky mound of her flesh. I was snug and safe, but the sobs still continued to rip out of me. When they had finally gasped to a trickle and then tailed to pitiful, whimpering sniffs, I raised my face, wiping a smudge of tears and snail-slime snot across Florence's bosom. Nobody, apart from Florence, seemed to have moved and Beatrice and Char-les stared at me with eyes of both amazement and fear. The smear of contempt was still frozen across Onyango's features but his eyes were also wide with amazement.

'I am sorry. Please forgive me.' I spoke the words at Onyango, and there could be no doubt about the regret and hopeless misery slumped in my voice. His eyes narrowed, lost their sparkle, widened again and then he smiled.

'How can you show me that you are sorry, imperious little spy at the window?'

I shrugged and gulped helplessly. I could still feel the warm trickles of snot trailed across my cheek and the rising bubbles of hot tears aching behind my eyes. I rubbed at my left cheek with the back of my hand.

'I don't know. What do you want me to do?' I let my pink, swollen gaze drift to Beatrice, Char-les and Florence. Florence had now released me from her huge embrace and was standing a pace or two from me with her massive arms folded. All three were looking at Onyango, and he was looking at me. His smile was still wrapped across his face and it seemed to be a calculating, greedy smile to me, but anything was better than the previous contempt.

'Come home with me now.'

'What? How? What do you mean?'

'Come home with me now. Now. Leave with us. Come to my home. Not my home at the lake, but the place where I stay here. Come home with me and see how life is outside these sacred, superior walls of your foolish safety.'

I looked at the other three. Not a muscle moved in Char-les' face and I wondered, with some strange, remote corner of my mind that had switched off from the scene, whether he understood English at all. Beatrice and Florence stared at Onyango; faint whispers of gasps fluttered from their sagging lips.

'I can't. You know I can't. Oh, please!' Onyango shrugged his shoulders against the door frame. His smudges of dark eyebrows twitched briefly upwards.

'Not that sorry then, little spy at the window? Not sorry enough to come to the home of a stinking, lazy black?' He half turned, rolling his body on the door jamb as though he was leaving.

'Wait. What about tomorrow? I'll come tomorrow. Won't that be the same?'

'When tomorrow?'

'Whenever you want. Tomorrow night? After dinner? After lunch? After breakfast?'

'And you'll stay the night in the home of a stinking, lazy black?'

The silence was as fragile as spider silk. I let its tension linger in the still silence of the kitchen for only a fraction of a second.

'Yes. Yes.' A sigh rose up from the depths of Beatrice, Florence and even Char-les like a moan. Onyango only smiled, however, but his smile was like a victory fanfare, and his eyes held mine and the triumph in them made them glow like treacle.

'Come outside and promise that to your god,' he said quietly.

'I promise, I promise.' I hurled the words away from me as though they hurt, slinging them out before I could change my mind.

'No. Come outside into the garden so that your god in the sky can hear you and take note.'

The garden air in the night was soft and hot. The stars in the clear, immense sky seemed to burn with the huge consuming fever of desperate promises. Charles, Beatrice and Florence gathered in the kitchen doorway and watched as Onyango and I stood barefoot on the dry grass. In his left hand Onyango took my right hand, and with his right hand he pointed upwards to the sparkling endlessness.

'Promise,' he said. His voice was soft and urgent and was so close to my ear that I could feel his lips ruffling the wisps of my hair.

'I promise,' I murmured, and then, because I knew it would please him, I repeated it loudly, almost as a shout. 'I promise.'

Still holding my hand, Onyango looked down into my face. His treacle eyes met mine in a smile of pleased complicity. He paused, dropped my hand and then turned to the wide-eyed, fearful watchers in the doorway. 'Come on, we're late already. Aren't you ready to go?'

They scurried after him then, frightened, quiet hurry in their faces; their eyes did not meet mine. I went back to the kitchen doorway and looked out into the night. They were already out of sight, but I could hear the jabber of their frantic, hasty, excited voices heading away from me. They were not speaking English, but I nevertheless knew, of course, what they were talking about.

I shut the kitchen door and turned out the lights. In my bed again, sleep swamped me rapidly, folding me in a huge cloud of black obliteration.

Chapter Nine

Mr Ballantine came for lunch and Dr Cairns came for afternoon tea. Dr Cairns came alone, for Richard and Andrew were busy examining a pile of samples somewhere. All the time I felt a hot-and-cold mixture of eager, anticipatory dread. It made me chatter in short nervous bursts and then lapse into an anxious silence. It made me approach mealtimes with a ferocious, nibbling, rodent greed until I quickly felt so uncomfortably full and flatulent that I wondered if I might have contracted Richard's stomach complaint.

Beatrice came up to me on silent, gliding feet as I stood in the garden when Dr Cairns had left after tea. I was lost in the heat of the sun on my back and in the contemplation of the flimsy length of the jasmine tendrils. I was keeping my racing mind a reassuring blank. I had avoided the kitchen the way the house servants had avoided meeting my eyes. We knew, we were afraid, and we knew we were afraid.

'Onyango is waiting for you by the front gate in five minutes.' Her expression was a carefully balanced neutral and her eyes were averted from my face, gazing downwards at my hands. I looked down at my hands too, and to my surprise I noticed that they were leading a separate, nervous existence of their own. They were shredding and rolling a small tatter of leaf. It was a limp green vestige of rag in my thin stubby fingers. I dropped it hastily on to the ground as though it might be interpreted as incriminating evidence.

'What about dinner?'

'Onyango will give you dinner.'

'No. Dinner here. What if somebody comes? Dr Cairns or Mr Ballantine?'

'Nobody will come.' She seemed very sure of this, for there was not a fragment of uncertainty in the placid serenity of her reply, despite the worry in her eyes.

'What do I need to take with me?'

'Nothing is needed.'

'Nothing?' A barely perceptible nod just glimpsed out of the corner of my downwards staring, unseeing eyes answered me. There was nothing else for either of us to say. Perhaps she might have said 'goodbye' or 'good luck', but both would have sounded foolish and false in the bright, wide heat and light of the afternoon. Instead we walked away from the jasmine bush in the garden in opposite directions. Beatrice returned in her lithe, elegant stride towards the kitchen and I, trying to saunter casually, headed down the crunching drive, the gravel glittering in the sun like wicked, knowing eyes, to the front gate.

It took about half an hour to reach the place where Onyango stayed. We walked in silence broken only by the slap of our feet on the track. Onyango strode ahead of me, barefoot and arrogant in the red dust. He had his cap on back to front, so that the peak covered the back of his neck. I followed him meekly without trying to talk to him. I could feel the sun biting into me and sweat sliding greasily down my back. He walked fast, and I had to jerk into snatches of stumbling running to keep up. My shoes were hurting, pinching my toes together and rubbing my heels into raw blisters. I felt he had made his point even before we had arrived.

Onyango's home was visible from the track. A short beaten path separated the wide dusty strip from an uneven cluster of a dozen or so round mud huts. Before we approached them he turned, paused in his stride and smiled at me. I looked down awkwardly at

131

my shoes covered in a film of the red dust from the track. I was ashamed and I was afraid, and my fear made me further ashamed. He raised my face by the pressure of his forefinger under my chin. I jerked my head up quickly at his touch and met his eyes. There was all the triumph and arrogance of before shining in them, but to my surprise their treacly glow seemed kind and gentle too, and his smile held friendship and, more surprisingly, admiration.

'We have arrived, little spy at the window.' He dropped his hand from my chin and swung away from me. He strode up the narrow path towards the huts and I followed at my scurrying, meek and respectful distance.

There were a couple of thin, scrawny hens scratching in the dirt outside the huts and one even scrawnier, thinner dog with yellow eyes, distended teats and a shining grey bald patch on one of her back legs. The dog whined hopefully as we approached and gave a hoarse semi-bark, but she also cringed away as though accustomed to being kicked. Small fires burned thinly and smokily outside two of the huts. Other than that there was no evidence of humanity. Onyango strode into the centre of the group of dwellings and barked some order into the hot blue emptiness.

He turned to me. 'How do you like it, little spy at the window? Do you like the mud walls and thatch, straw roofs? How do you feel about the spacious kitchen?' He jerked his thumb towards one of the small fires. 'Would you like to live here?'

Dark eyes appeared at the doorway to one of the mud huts, and a little girl poked herself out. She was perhaps seven, maybe younger, maybe older, and she carried a pot-bellied naked baby boy on one hip. She appeared to be answering Onyango's shouted summons, for she looked at him both warily and obediently.

132

Onyango impatiently beckoned her out of the door-way. As she emerged from the shadowed gloom into the bright sun, other eyes appeared behind her and followed her out. A squawking, rattling, pointing and giggling muddle of nine or ten children in a ragtag assembly of semi-dress. None of them had shoes on and the clothes that they wore all seemed dirty and tattered and much too big or much too small for them. They looked like the children that followed us in squealing, wheeling loops when we drove to Max's church every Sunday, but the church was in the opposite direction.

The little girl with the baby on her hip appeared to be the oldest and in charge. I was nervously eager to make the right impression and show that my behaviour of the previous day had been a fluke. I took a small step towards her and said '*Jambo!*' She stared back at me silently, but although one or two of the other children ran quickly back into the hut, most of the scamper of ragged urchins behind her immediately burst into squawks of jabbering delight and amuse-ment. I could hear them imitating my thin, stiff voice in their excited chatter and they giggled all the more at their mimicry and stuffed the corners of their grubby clothes into their mouths and pointed at me.

Onyango snapped some words at them, and apart from stray grins and giggles they became quiet and watchful. He threw a few more words at the little girl and she nodded and pointed, stretching her arm in the direction in which we were walking up the track, but she kept her huge, fascinated eyes fixed on me. Another scattering of words was thrown at her and I felt the helpless fear of being the only one who did not under-stand. The words 'I am a stranger in a strange land' rose from some unknown, dusty recess in my mind.

'This way.' Onyango was walking away from me, leaving me standing foolishly on my own. The yellow-eyed dog was fawning around my feet and I followed

Onyango quickly. I did not want my skin to touch the limp, mangy fur of the dog.

'This is where I stay' He had stopped outside the doorway of the hut furthest from the central grouping. It looked like all the others to me: round, windowless, and with the thatched straw roof drooping in a tatty fringe over the edges of the mud walls. The wooden door was closed and appeared to me to bear the bruises of a history of kicking.

'It's very nice,' I said. Onyango gave me a jeering glance of amusement and disbelief.

'Oh yes?' and he added some other words that I did not understand to someone behind me. I turned around quickly. One of the little boys was staggering up behind us carrying a large chair in his arms. The chair was wooden with a leather seat. It was much too big for the small boy to manage easily and it was banging off his thin shins with every step. He did not even appear to notice. He put it down carefully where Onyango indicated, just to the left of the doorway of the hut, and then scampered back to where the scuffling group of children was watching us from a safe distance. He dived in amongst them as though he was escaping, which indeed he appeared to have done, for he was immediately indistinguishable to me amongst the giggling huddle of children's excited faces.

Onyango opened the door of the hut and for the first time indicated that I should go ahead of him. There was a raised earth lip to the doorway and I felt a strange and indefinable thrill of adventure as I stepped across it. He wedged the door open with a chunk of stone and the bright afternoon sun streamed with disconcerting solidity into the shadows of the dark interior. I was surprised by the spartan cleanliness inside Onyango's home: one single bed which appeared almost military in the neat precision of its folded blanket, one ragged, chewed cardboard box

134

that seemed to contain clothes, one stool and one small table. The hard earth floor was clean and his machete, which he called a panga, was hanging from a nail on the wall and glittered brightly and ferociously in the sudden stream of sunlight.

There were two books on the table, one on top of the other. Both were thick and ragged and both had the grey pallor of boredom and age. I wondered what the books were and who read them, but I didn't touch. Restraining my curious hands reminded me suddenly of Aunt Bernice in the incredible, invisible distance of Cornwall. It was a sad, lonely, frightened thought that made me flinch as though it had suddenly crept up and punched me.

'Is something wrong?'

'No. No. It's very nice here.'

'Oh yes?' Again the amusement and disbelief. 'Come outside and sit down.'

I sat in the huge, grand chair by the door to Onyango's hut and he gave me a dented tin mug of water to drink. Then he brought the two books out of his hut and placed them carefully on the ground beside me.

'I have to go and see someone now. I'll be about an hour. Here are my books in case you are bored. Beatrice and Florence have told me how you like to read.' He paused and then added, 'And I will be very angry if you throw them around.' Was every action in Marsdon Villas reported and discussed, I wondered. Before I could even consider asking, Onyango had gone, striding quickly away from me towards the track without looking back. I was left with only a worn-out cur, a couple of chickens and a straggle of ragged children for company in the hot, hot sun of the afternoon.

Onyango was gone for much longer than an hour, and I remembered some comments that Mr Ballantine had made that lunch time to me about different

135

concepts of time. I remembered with a restless anxiety however, for I felt not only bored, but very foolish. The children gathered around me and squatted on their haunches in a rough semi-circle on the dry earth, beaten to a concrete hardness by the passage of countless feet. They stared at me with eyes as unrelenting as the sun, as though I was a fascinating, but unpredictably dangerous beast, for they kept themselves at a wary distance.

The scrawny dog with yellow eyes came and festered at my feet. I shrank away from any contact with her pitiful yellow fur, drawing my feet backwards under the chair away from her. She pushed her long ferret face under the chair however, snuffling at my ankles, and I kicked out at her half-heartedly in an attempt to frighten her away. My foot caught her almost imperceptibly on her right ear, barely grazing the lone spikes of rank hair that tufted from its tip. She cringed backwards, whining and yelping, as though I had struck her firmly in the face. The children screamed and hooted with pitiless mirth and the little girl with the naked, round-bellied baby still clasped to her hip came forward. She pulled the dog away from me by its thin yellow tail that seemed to be covered in scales rather than fur. The dog snapped at her in an abject attempt at ferocity and she kicked it hard in the belly with her bare, splay-toed feet. The dog cringed away, lay down in the shade of Onyango's hut and chewed on her own distended teats. Flies clustered about her, but she made no effort to flick them away.

The children continued to stare at me with their huge, curious eyes. Seated uncomfortably in my throne-like chair I felt like a strange royalty holding court over ranks of subjects who ultimately controlled me. It was an unpleasant, humiliating feeling and I was thankful that at least the scrawny chickens showed no interest in me.

The time passed achingly slowly. I smiled hopefully

at the circle of children. I was too discouraged by my last attempt to try speaking to them in my faltering Swahili. They did not smile back, but pointed at me and giggled nervously. One little boy, I thought he could perhaps have been the chair-carrier, darted forward in his flapping grey shirt and torn blue shorts, and touched my bare arm briefly with his filthy fore-finger. He looked at his finger and then held it up for the other children to see. The little girl came forward again and yanked him backwards by his scraggy arm. She swiped a clumsy blow at him with the back of her hand, and although she caught him on the cheek it was not a hard hit, hindered as she was by the baby on her hip. She was the first to examine more closely the finger that had touched my arm.

After that, the children kept their wide-eyed, staring distance and I turned my attention to the two tomes that Onyango had left me for my entertainment. One was a Gray's *Anatomy* and the other was an English dictionary. I wondered where and how Onyango had acquired these weighty volumes and whether he could read. Perhaps he had developed his vocabulary from reading the dictionary; I quickly found that a definition of catamite was included. My earlier difficulties with that word impelled me to leave the treasures of medical knowledge and curious diagrams of Gray's *Anatomy*, and as I waited through the long heat of the afternoon for Onyango to return, under the scrutiny of the tussle of restless children and the yellow eyes of the threadbare dog, I read the dictionary.

Onyango returned in the brief minutes of the tropical dusk. The children scattered from him as he strode up towards us and he threw angry, snapping shouts towards their backs. He kicked at the bony rump of the prostrated yellow-eyed dog and it scurried, yelping and cringing, after the children. Then he turned and looked at me where I sat on my wooden throne. I empathized with the yellow-eyed dog then, for I too

137

felt like yelping and cringing under that cold, long, judgemental stare. He smiled, and his eyes became warm, treacle pools and I gave an answering, nervous smile up into his face.

'You look afraid, little spy at the window.'

'No.'

'Good. Come inside now. It is almost night time. The other people who live here will soon be back from their hard day of toil.'

He followed me into the hut carrying my huge wooden throne of the afternoon with him. I carried the two books and the empty tin mug. I put them gently on the table.

'You were bored?'

'No.'

He had taken the stump of a candle from some hiding place in a recess of the roof thatch. He lit it and shut the door and our huge shadows danced and bounced across the room and were swallowed into the darkness.

'Sit down.' I perched again on the edge of the throne and Onyango pushed the wooden stool up close and sat facing me. Half his face glowed in the candlelight and the other half was lost in shadow. I could smell a warm, malty, fermented scent on his breath. It reminded me of Cornish fields in the summertime and grizzled old men reeling out of sea-front public houses at Christmas.

'You have been drinking?'

'What drink could a lazy humble black like me be imbibing?'

'That stuff that you make.' He laughed, a short, curt hard laugh.

'I see that my little spy at the window may be stupid, but is not entirely ignorant.'

The one eye of his that I could see, looked huge and tawny and beautiful. It moved closer and closer towards me. When he kissed me with his warm, wet, wide lips and I could taste, rather than just smell, the alcohol in his breath, I neither flinched nor resisted.

After a while Onyango sat back from me. He stood up and went out of the hut. The candle flame flickered in the draught from the opening door, and my immense shadow bobbed in a dance of mockery across the rough adobe walls. It was dark outside and I could hear the crackle and murmur of adult voices drifting through the shadows and woodsmoke. I cringed at the thought of having to meet the owners of those voices with their respectfully blank faces and their knowing eyes lit with the confidence of being on their own territory. I shifted and wriggled uncomfortably on the slippery leather seat of my throne; if I had ever felt that I had any control over my life's events, it certainly was not now.

Onyango was gone for only a matter of minutes. Again the candle flame flickered and my startled shadow leapt anxiously up the walls as the door opened with his return. I knew at once that he was not alone, but the person with him was momentarily masked by the sturdy width of his body.

'You should stand up, my sweet little spy at the window, when your elders and betters come into the room.' I slithered from the chair on to my feet and the person with Onyango appeared from behind him.

She was a crumpled, wizened old woman, bald apart from a few tufts of wiry grey curls and her eyes watery and pink. As her mouth twisted into a brief grimace of a grin, I glimpsed an assortment of black stumps of teeth. Her skin hung on her limbs in loose wrinkled folds as though devoid of internal flesh, and where her torn grubby dress gaped open at the front I could see the flat, empty pouches of her breasts, hanging like the discarded flaps of balloons, shrunken and flabby with age. I had never seen a black person so old and worn, but she seemed neither crumbling nor decrepit. She scurried forward from behind Onyango with the eagerness of a young terrier. She scampered towards me chattering rapidly and shrilly, but with her body stooped and her hands outstretched in a gesture of obeisance.

She took my hand, which I had stretched out towards her for a formal handshake, in both of hers and seemed prepared to creak to her elderly knees to kowtow to me. I resisted her genuflecting movements by catching her right hand in both of mine and pulling upwards.

Her hands in mine were wrinkled, leathery and scarred. The skin seemed almost inanimate in its toughness. She seemed pleased by this mutual gesture of clasped hands and grinned at me broadly, revealing again the mottled shining pink of her gums. Her rheumy, veined eyes glittering in the candlelight appeared manic and evil. She twitched her balding head towards Onyango and crackled a stream of incomprehensible words at him.

'She says that you are very beautiful. She is telling you to sit down. She is going to bring us dinner.'

I stood there smiling awkwardly at the old lady. She cackled and nodded her head encouragingly. Our hands were still clasped together.

'Sit down then.'

Onyango sounded impatient and tense. I gently released my hands from the old woman's wrinkled, coriaceous grasp and sat down again on the throne. My face was aching from the effort of keeping my beaming smile ever-widening on my face. Still cackling to herself and talking to Onyango, the woman crouched by his bed and felt underneath it with her scrawny arms extended. Onyango made no effort either to help her or respond to her stream of chatter, but moved the stool away from me to the other side of the table, and sat down. He leant back against the wall and stretched his long legs out into the centre of the hut. His eyes were semi-closed into laconic slits and his posture reminded me of the stippled geckos basking in the sun around Marsdon Villas. Still chattering to either Onyango or herself, the old lady scurried out of the hut on her broad bare feet. She clutched to her deflated bosom a number of empty dishes that she had retrieved from beneath the bed.

She returned in a few minutes. In her short absence neither I nor Onyango had spoken or moved. She was carrying the largest dish in her outstretched arms. It was half full of water which sloshed against the sides as she walked. She proffered the bowl to me. I looked at it uncertainly, then at the old woman and then at Onyango. He was still slumped nonchalantly against the wall, but I could see his lazy eyes had flicked towards me and he was watching me. I was afraid that I might make an appalling, ritualistic mistake. It would be terrible to wash in water that was intended for drinking.

'Wash your hands.'

There was impatience again in Onyango's voice and I wondered if my ignorance might be embarrassing him in front of this old lady to whom he had shown such minimal respect, despite his earlier words about elders and betters. I dipped my hands into the water, and it felt cool and silky running between my anxious, sweating fingers. I shook the drips from them and looking briefly into the water's surface I saw my pale, worried reflection shimmering and breaking in the concentric circles of the splashes.

Onyango only washed his right hand, quickly, splashily, and the drops of water he shook from it caught the light from the candle, giving a momentary impression that a burnished rainbow flew from his fingertips.

The old woman left us to eat alone. One plate, one bowl and two battered mugs of water on the table divided us.

'*Karibu*,' grinned Onyango, inviting me to eat. I

141

knew that he was mocking my uncertainty about how to tackle the meal. The plate held a steaming mound of a grey, doughy substance. I recognized from the tattered threads of half-forgotten conversations with Mr Ballantine that this was *ugali*: maize flour mixed with boiling water and beaten to a glutinous stodge. The bowl was almost half full of a yellow liquid, whose surface shimmered with a layer of grease. Fibrous shreds of meat were visible floating in the oily depths and one scaly yellow chicken's foot, the toes of the claw folded inwards as though clutching at some unseen straw of hope. I wondered if this offering was from one of the disdainful chickens that I had seen scratching outside the huts in the afternoon. My hand hovered nervously over the *ugali*, unsure of how to begin.

'Which hand?' hissed Onyango across the table, as though unseen judges might be observing my efforts and he must not be detected helping me. It was not the first time that I had wished I was not left-handed. I stalled and Onyango started on the meal. He tore a chunk of *ugali* from the mound with his right hand and moulded and squeezed it expertly in his fist. With the right thumb he indented a scoop-like hollow in his sculpture which he dipped into the yellow chicken broth and then moved quickly to his mouth. Both the *ugali* and the scoop of the soup were consumed in one mouthful and the whole sequence of movements was completed in seconds.

I tried to imitate him using my fumbling right hand; the *ugali* was scorchingly hot and burned me, and the fragment that I managed to pull from the mound was small and crumbly. As I rolled and squeezed it, it stuck itself between my fingers and under my nails. The thumb-scoop hollow cracked and flaked and the warm greasy liquid slid up my wrist and arm as I delivered the hard-won morsel of unattractive food to my suspicious mouth. It did not have so much an

142

unpleasant taste, as no taste at all. It was bland and insipid and the texture was a disagreeable mixture of the oily and the gritty. Onyango watched my clumsy copy of his eating technique with undisguised amusement.

'Do you like this humble meal of the lazy ignorant black?'

'It is very nice. Thank you. Very hot too.'

I breathed out clouds of steam across the table. Onyango smiled at me. We continued eating our meal in silence. Although my technique of moulding the *ugali* with one hand quickly improved, the taste, or rather the consistency, of each cloying mouthful seemed to become increasingly unpleasant and my rapidly palling enthusiasm for the meal was soon satiated entirely. I stopped eating and rubbed my chicken-slime-smeared mouth with the back of my hand. Onyango had excavated away at least half of the *ugali* mound facing him. The quarrying on my side was a paltry nibbling in comparison.

'That was delicious.' I tried to display both appreciation and a firm finality in my voice. Onyango raised his eyebrows questioningly.

'You have hardly eaten anything.'

'I have,' I protested, 'and I'm full now.'

'What about this? This is for you, too.'

With his right hand again, Onyango dipped into the murky depths of the soup bowl and fished out the chicken's foot. The pimply skin at the torn end hung in loose, saggy folds like an oversized stocking and dripped yellow watery chicken grease on the table. He waved the claw in front of me and the reptilian toes seemed to be grasping forward like menacing talons.

'You have it. I'm not hungry,' I said hastily, and then after a brief pause, added, 'thank you.'

Onyango shrugged again. If he was considering humiliating me by shaming me into attempting to gnaw on this grotesque chicken claw, his own greed outweighed his plans. He chewed into it eagerly, spitting the short bones out on to the table without self-consciousness.

He appeared almost demonic, with the greasy chicken's foot clutched in his right hand, his dark eyes glowing in the candlelight and the slick of oily fat gleaming around his lips. I watched him with fascination as he devoured the food; it seemed only a matter of time before he started on me. Events appeared to be bewitched and I felt that my wishes, if I had any, were futile. I made no effort to control, or even manipulate, the flow of circumstances.

When he had finished cleaning the last shred of flesh from the bones of the chicken foot, Onyango stood up, stretched himself like a lazy, satisfied cat and went to the door of the hut. He barked some command impatiently into the surrounding darkness. A thin voice from the night answered him, and shortly afterwards the old woman returned carrying the hand-washing basin, slopping with clean water. We washed our grease-smeared hands and faces in the water, and to my surprise the water was tepid and had a hint of soapiness. The woman continued her guttural chattering to Onyango, jerking her head between the detritus on the table and me.

'She is asking why you don't like her meal.'

'I do like it, very much. I'm just not hungry,' I protested again. Onyango seemed to translate what I had said, and my feeble excuses appeared to satisfy the woman, for she nodded and grinned at me, revealing again the hideous sculpture of her teeth. She threw the washing water outside the door of the hut in a careless slosh, and placed the half-finished dishes of *ugali* and chicken slime into the empty bowl. With a damp rag in her hand, that now reminded me uncomfortably of the chicken claw that Onyango had so voraciously consumed, she swept the debris and slops of the meal from the table into the bowl. The crumbs of *ugali*, the

144

shining ivory bones spat from Onyango's wide lips, the dribbles of greasy liquid, all smudged together as discarded waste.

She muttered again at Onyango, grinned and then scurried out of the door with the wreckage of our meal clutched tightly in her shrivelled arms. Onyango followed her to the doorway and stood on the raised earth lip of the entrance, rocking gently backwards and forwards on the balls of his bare feet and gazing out into the soft, smoky darkness.

'She says it is going to rain, so she is bringing water to wash in now.'

'Oh.'

He returned to the table, leaving the door hanging open to the warm emptiness of the night. He scrutinized me as though I was a specimen of some interest, looking down at me as I still sat on my uncomfortable throne. He smiled, and the candlelight bounced off his shining teeth.

'Then, my little spy at the window, it will be bedtime.'

I shrugged and smiled. There was nothing for me to say. I was, I felt, a helpless pawn in a game that, like chess, I did not understand.

The old lady was standing in the doorway once again. She was carrying the washing bowl carefully, and I could see that it was full almost to the brim with gently steaming water and was heavy on her thin arm. She did not come in, but hurled some words at Onyango and grinned her ancient, ugly grin at me, jerking her head backwards on her withered neck.

'Go with her.'

Obediently I stood up and followed the old lady outside. I wondered if I should offer to carry the bowl for her, but I knew that my young arms would be weaker than her old ones, and I remained silent. I could see why she had predicted rain, for the air was hot, heavy and thunderily oppressive, and low rolling clouds had obliterated the endless stretches of stars. In the hut I had considered that the air's stuffy humidity was a symptom of my anxiety rather than a reflection of the weather; now I was not so sure.

She walked around to the back of Onyango's hut. I followed close behind her, for it was very dark in the starless night. The only visible illumination came from the small cooking fires by the main cluster of huts and the occasional green-yellow glimpse of light from fireflies.

With careful precision the old woman crouched and placed the bowl of steaming water on the ground, making only a few splashes. She then produced, from what seemed to be under the sagging flap of her left breast, a tiny stump of candle, which she lit. She stood back from the bowl, holding the candle in front of her in the manner of an unlikely chorister, and looked at me. I hesitated, unsure of what to do. She cackled noisily, and to my surprise pointed at a nearby clump of euphorbia, its ragged branches casting lumpy shadows in the flickering light of the candle. I frowned in puzzlement and shook my head, and she punched a few unintelligible sentences at me. I shook my head again, and shrugged.

'I don't understand,' but there was nobody there to translate for either of us.

She squatted then, down on her thin scraggy legs, her knees bent apart and her dress bunched up around her waist. Through the few stumps of her teeth she made a pronounced hissing whistle. She straightened up, grinned and pointed first at me and then at the euphorbia. There was no mistaking this grotesque pantomime, and I felt a relieved gratitude as I nodded and walked deliberately over to the euphorbia bush.

The woman followed me, holding the candle up high to cast a pool of light on the ground ahead of me. I paused and she paused also. Surely she was not going to stand and watch me? She nodded encouragingly

146

and I smiled back nervously. She crouched again in her coarse, ludicrous parody complete with sound effects, and again stood up and nodded encouragingly. I nodded in reply to try to convey to her that I understood. She obviously doubted this however, for she seemed to be about to start a third burlesque rendition, when I forestalled her. I was clearly going to have to perform in front of her, under the gathering rain clouds and in the flicker of the candlelight, and I wanted to stop this farce of nodding and smiling now and get it over with quickly. I took a couple of steps back from her and crouching under the feeble branches of the euphorbia, urinated.

The ground was too hard and dry for instant absorption, and I cringed as my streams of urine, and despite the day's heat there was no small amount, flowed, as though on purpose, towards the bare, cracked feet of my audience. She shifted sideways and out of the way just in time. I was rewarded with one of her hideous grins and such a riot of nodding that I was afraid that her leering monkey skull might become detached from her scrawny neck.

Still nodding and grinning she led me back to the bowl of water. Washing also took place under her watery, bright gaze and chuckle, but unlike Beatrice or the children she appeared to have no wish to touch the expanses of sickly pale flesh that I revealed before her in the candle's glimmer. I was grateful for this, for I felt sure that if she had been curious she would have had no qualms about a few investigative prods.

When I had washed, and dried myself on a stretch of dry coarse cloth that she seemed to pluck mysteriously out of the night darkness, she led me back to the door of Onyango's hut. She pinched the candle out in the doorway and thrust it back down the torn cleavage of her dress. She then took my hand in both her talons and fired a short gabble of speech at me which ended with a vulgar shout of laughter. It was totally incomprehensible to me, of course, so I merely smiled politely and said,

'Thank you. Good night.'

As she scuttled off in the darkness towards the glow of the fires at the cluster of huts, like some crazy moth still chuckling crudely to herself, I slid back into the candlelit relative safety and sanity of Onyango's hut. My neck ached from so much nodding and my cheeks from so much desperate smiling.

Onyango had taken off his shirt and stood barechested and gleaming in the candlelight. There was a long narrow scar across his chest that I had not noticed before and it seemed to be inviting my finger to trace its path. His muscles appeared to be rippling in the uncertain yellow light of the flame, which was wavering in the draught from the closing door. His cap lay upside down on the table and his short scrolls of hair also glinted blackly in the light.

'Get into bed,' he commanded imperiously, 'I am going to wash.' He strode arrogantly out of the hut. I finished my mug of water which had been left on the table. The water was tepid and seemed to stick in my mouth, giving no refreshment.

I undressed down to my white, scared underwear, placing my clothes carefully across the back of my afternoon throne. Barefoot, I scuttled across the floor, my shadow, like a huge cockroach, following me, bouncing across the thatch. The blanket on the bed was rough and smelt, not unpleasantly, of sweat and sunshine. I huddled against the wall and could also smell the mustiness of grass and mud in the adobe bricks. Outside I could hear the hard, sharp bursts of Onyango urinating, and the slop and ringing splash of water on metal as he washed.

He came back into the hut and I lay rigidly still in bed, pretending to be asleep. Until I heard him bolting the door on the inside I had hoped, half-desperately, half-regretfully, that he was going to sleep in another

148

hut. I heard his ragged trousers slide to the floor, and from the corner of my half-opened eye I could see that he was completely naked. He pinched out the candle between his finger and thumb and slid into the narrow bed beside me. The warm flesh of his upper leg touched mine, and in spite of myself, I turned towards him.

Despite his arrogance, anger and imperious contempt he was very gentle as he finished undressing me. Despite the fear and the pain there was also pleasure, and not least was the pleasure that for perhaps the first time in my life I felt both wanted and appreciated, and that I could also be a source of pleasure.

When I finally slept, much later, sprawled in a muddle of limbs and coarse hairy blanket, my dreams were tangled and confused. I dreamt that I was reading a book of poetry. The poems were unknown to me and I was reading them behind the thundering curtain of a waterfall. As I finished each page of the book I ripped it out and held the flimsy white rectangle of printed paper out into the torrent of water. The water tore each sheet from my hand and sucked it into oblivion. I tried to watch each diminishing page of white as the rush of water bore it away, but the flow was so rapid that they disappeared almost as soon as they were torn from my hand.

I woke up suddenly, but the thundering of the waterfall still continued, and I realized that it was raining, the torrential heavy rain of a tropical storm. My left arm was uncomfortable under the weight of Onyango's sleep-heavy body, and as I wriggled it out, he woke up. The thundering of the rain on the thatch and the dreamy waterfall merged, and this time the pain was less and the pleasure more.

An insistent rattling and banging of the door and loud, urgent shouting clamouring above the hammer of the rain woke us both up.

'What is it?' called Onyango sleepily in English, and

the urgent voice repeated its message, unintelligible to me.

'Get up, get up,' snapped Onyango, and the urgency had transferred itself to his voice, dispelling all signs of sleep.

'There are white people here and looking for you.'

We were both hastily out of bed and I was pulling on my clothes that I had draped across the throne chair. I was fumbling for my underwear, discarded in a tangle by the side of the bed, when the door was rattled again.

'Zag, are you there? We know you are. Open the door.' It was Mr Hannett's imperious voice, and behind him, but still audible over the ceaseless thumping of the rain, I could hear the discordant, high-pitched whine of his wife.

'This is just too disgusting!'

Onyango clamped his hand across my mouth, but an automatic 'Yes' had already escaped me. Onyango threw me an exasperated look in the dim gloom of the hut. He had his trousers on, but was still shirtless and his feet, as usual, were bare. He pulled his cap on and opened the door.

Within confused minutes I was being yanked into the grey, wet, misty gloom of a torrentially rainy dawn. The ground was a quagmire of glutinous red mud which was also spattered in dollops over the Hannetts' shoes and clothing. I had pulled on my shoes, but my knickers still lay crumpled somewhere near or under Onyango's bed. With a cold bare bottom under my dress, my feelings of vulnerability and disbelief were accentuated to nightmare proportions. Again submitting without a struggle to the whims of a querulous god of fate, I was propelled by the drenched and bedraggled Hannetts, one on either side of me, through the damp, squalid cluster of huts towards where their car waited on the dirt track, which now flowed with water.

Neither of them had uttered a word to either me or

150

Onyango, as they had snatched me from the gurry warmth of his hut. Their lips were compressed into thin lines of rage and ashamed incredulity. As we approached the car, there was a shrill yell behind us. Without a word we all stopped and turned. It was Onyango, running after us, the water bouncing off his still shirtless back. His left hand was raised aloft and in it something white was trailing through the raindrops. It was my missing pair of knickers.

He thrust them into my hands without a word, sneered briefly and silently into the Hannetts' bewildered, furious faces, and bolted quickly back to the shelter of his hut. Perhaps Mr Hannett thought it was a secret message, for he snatched the knickers, now damp from the rain, from my hand and held them up. As he realized what he was holding his bewilderment changed to horrified shock and the intensity of the fury etched on his face increased. He dropped, or more accurately hurled, the offending garment on to the swampy path and ground it with his heel into the oozing red mud.

Chapter Ten

Ocean View, Malindi, Kenya.
Dear Aunt Bernice,

Are you surprised by the new address? Ziggy, Marsdon and I have come to spend a few weeks on the coast relaxing. We are staying in a small bungalow that belongs to the Frobishers (you may remember that they are friends of Marsdon's family who came to visit at Marsdon Villas and that Mr Frobisher has an important government job in Nairobi). They have kindly said that we can stay here until Christmas if we wish, and it is so nice here that we might do so. We have the Frobishers' elderly housewoman to cook our meals and wash our clothes, but I do some small duties around the house as well.

It is so nice to be near the sea again. I had forgotten how much I like to be near it. The house is right by the beach which is beautiful, clean white coral sand and fringed with coconut palms. I am sitting on the beach as I write this letter. The Indian Ocean is so warm compared to the sea off Cornwall and we stay in the water for hours. Marsdon and Ziggy have been taken snorkelling on the coral reef recently, and the fish that they have described to me sound wonderful. I am sure I will have a chance to go with them before we leave here, which will be very exciting.

The Frobishers may come down for a weekend to visit, but unfortunately Max, Lily and the Hannetts are too busy at Marsdon Villas to join us. However, there are a number of white people who have houses here and although we have not yet been to dinner *with any of them they are keeping an eye on us.*

I hope that you are well. Despite being lucky enough to go on this seaside holiday, I have not forgotten Cornwall and I include you in my prayers every night. I am sure that Ziggy will write to you soon. He has so much to tell you about his stay in Nanyuki etc. Yours lovingly, Zag.

Another letter in which economy with facts and a host of sugared semi-truths jostled together. I could not imagine that Ziggy had even considered writing to Aunt Bernice. I lay back in the sand. If nothing else, at least my descriptions of the scenery tended to be realistic. I turned my head and squinted into the sun; further up the beach I could see Ziggy and Marsdon jostling by the water's edge. In silhouette against the glare of the late morning, they could have been negroes. It seemed unfair that things which were indistinguishable at a distance, should only receive judgement after painfully close inspection.

All the same, things had not turned out so badly. At least, not for me. Here I was, lounging indolently on a beautiful tropical beach, and apart from the ever-awkward, paunchy Marsdon, my company was provided exclusively by my glorious golden brother, Ziggy.

The only problem was that Ziggy was furious with me. We had been staying at Ocean View for nearly a week, and still the only direct communication I had with him were narrow-eyed stares, laden with animosity. Spoken communication was accomplished when necessary, which was seldom, through Marsdon. Marsdon, with his spluttering stammer and his relentless bumbling awkwardness, did not make a good negotiator. I closed my eyes, and like unerasable nightmare sequences, images of the impact my one-night, unforgivable misdemeanour had made on the flow of life at Marsdon Villas danced mockingly before my eyes.

153

When we had arrived back at Marsdon Villas, the
Hannetts and I, slewing through the glutinous slithering mud of the track which sprayed the car in a casing
of ugly blood-red, the grey, wet dawn was blinking
through the rain into a grey, wet morning.

I had been sent straight to my room, but already I
had noticed that there were other vehicles parked in
the drive. The party from Nanyuki were back. Later I
found out that the forecast of torrential rain had caused
both the Hannetts and Marsdon's family, together with
Ziggy and Arabella, to drive back to Marsdon Villas
through the night. Torrential rain after weeks of such
dryness could have made the roads impassable with
floods and earth slides. At the time, however, the
unexpected appearance of what seemed like everybody was both horrific and bizarre. I would not have
been very much more surprised to have chanced upon
Aunt Bernice's face, wrinkled into a disapproving
grimace, peering down at me from amongst the heads
of stuffed animals which lined the landing.

I had left the door of my room ajar just a crack, but
the voices which screeched and bellowed from the
room below, where my fate was being decided, were
so magnified by rage and horror that I would probably
have heard them if I had closed my door firmly and
buried my head under the pillow. I stood by the
window and gazed out into the wet garden. The rain
fell like a solid sheet and there were no gardeners to
watch.

The images of my receiving judgement in the
drawing room later on in the morning, after I had been
brought breakfast in my room by a silent Florence who
would not look at me, were confused. Only a muddled
sequence of angry, accusing faces and voices becoming ever louder and ever shriller seethed in my
memory.

Max, swollen and purple like a prize kohlrabi, had

stamped and heaved about the room in his uneven gait. The crashing of the fat and angry clench of his fist against the wall boomed in the centre of my memories. Mr Hannett, his mouth a narrow, savage gash, seemed a vengeful sidekick. The wives of this pair of judge- mental furies squealed and screeched by turn, and from the corners of my conscience the silent eyes of indictment of Arabella, Marsdon and Ziggy glowered relentlessly.

They had wanted me to accuse Onyango of assault. Max in particular had tried to force me to do so by the oppressive volume of his voice. Amenable and in- capable as I was to the kicks and thrusts of fate, that was one act of falsity that I knew I was incapable of perpetrating. I buried my head in my arms and screwed my eyes shut to block out the ever-swelling roar of furious accusation and the glare of contemptu- ous, recriminatory eyes.

'No!' I had shouted out to the swirling, whirling mayhem, 'I wanted to. No, I wanted to!' I repeated myself again and again, louder and louder, trying to drown out the throb of anger, which despite being blocked out from my ears and eyes still beat endlessly and clamorously inside my head.

Somehow they had managed to summon Dr Cairns, and my behaviour with Onyango and my resultant hysteria were quickly decided to be some sort of psychiatric delirium. They had me strapped to my bed for the day, and I knew better than to question or refute their curious diagnosis which suited them so well. The atmosphere of contemptuous accusation was gradu- ally replaced by one of contemptuous pity, and Lily and Mrs Hannett made no attempt to disguise their long, supercilious conversations; the subject was always the distant whereabouts of my unfortunate mother.

Although face had been saved by this useful medical pronouncement about my mental health, my presence in Marsdon Villas was still an embarrassment of unguessable proportions. It was well known that snide remarks would soon cloud their sacred portals if I was not neatly disposed of. The gossip of servants can never be quenched, whatever the rules and punishments meted out. Nevertheless, I had clearly not been sufficiently unwell to be condemned to bed, and Dr Cairns had, wisely, refused to pretend that I was, although Max, Lily and the Hannetts had tried to persuade him otherwise.

Arguments had raged over dinner that evening, unabashed by the glitter of glass and silver cutlery and the white starched purity of the tablecloth. No effort seemed to be made to lower the volume of the discussion, and every heated word had been gusted up to me, and doubtless blew and sizzled into the cool ears of the kitchen. The problem of my presence was realized in every corner of Marsdon Villas.

If I had been sent back to Cornwall, then it would be clear to every expatriate in East Africa (so said Max) that I was a disgrace, rather than unwell. If the truth of the circumstances was revealed to Aunt Bernice it might have a disastrous effect on the state of her health (so said Ziggy), for she had shrivelled from merely elderly to old, and was likely to respond badly to shocks. It was stolid, lumpish Marsdon who had suggested that borrowing the Frobishers' coastal residence might be the solution, and once his stuttered suggestion had finally emerged through the angry din of outrage it was quickly seen as the answer. In Ocean View I could be out of the way until either the gossip had subsided or until it was time for Ziggy and I to return to England.

Dr Cairns was, for some reason, probably his austere and humourless voice and his medical authority, selected to telephone the Frobishers from the Tea Hotel in Kericho. He told them that I had become ill following an unspecified incident at Marsdon Villas and was in need of sea air and recuperation. The next day we had left Marsdon Villas, Kericho for Ocean View, Malindi on the Indian Ocean shores of Kenya.

Neither the Hannetts nor Max and Lily wanted or were able to accompany me in this exercise of recuperation and banishment, and Mrs Hannett refused to allow Arabella into the same room as me. Even if I was not sick, my ills were evidently both contagious and dangerous. It thus fell to Marsdon and Ziggy to be my guardians and chaperones on this trip to Malindi.

Marsdon, as ever, appeared stodgily indifferent at being forced into the role of nursemaid, but Ziggy was furious. He knew that I was neither mentally nor physically unwell, and he saw my behaviour as yet another disaster in my lifelong catalogue of fiascos and failures, that seemed to be purposefully designed to bring both disruption to his ordered life and ruin to his hopes and aspirations. Not only had I angered and upset everyone in Marsdon Villas, but I had also caused the separation of himself and Arabella. In the absence of Mr Ballantine, Ziggy had been advancing remarkably well in the favours of the beautiful Arabella, and now she was to be snatched away from him again. The guilt that had, since birth, swathed my relationship with Ziggy like impenetrable fog had increased again in its intensity, and I was not surprised by his refusal to speak to me.

Mr Ballantine had been persuaded to drive us to Nairobi to catch the night train to Mombasa. My memories of the journey were hazed with misery and exhaustion. One small image, however, remained lodged in my brain like a single line of an irritating song. Mr Ballantine had turned to me just outside Naivasha and given me a tired, hard stare. He had been driving and Marsdon and Ziggy had slumped asleep in the back seat, Marsdon snuffling and snoring as usual. I had kept steadfastly awake, as though punishing myself, and I had met Mr Ballantine's cold blue oriental gaze as steadily as I could. If he says 'don't say I didn't warn you . . .' I had thought, I will surely scream. Mr Ballantine had sighed, a patronizing, forgiving sigh.

'Don't say I didn't warn you . . .' he had murmured. I hadn't screamed, of course, but I had smiled a thin, strained smile at his predictability. His words implied that he also did not regard me as mentally unsound. He had frowned, however, at my wan smile.

'There's no reason to look so pleased with yourself either,' he snapped. 'You may not have wished to cause trouble, but you have. If you must embark on friendships with these people, then you must play the game of never being caught. Father Mannering has never been caught napping.'

Catamites again. I had wondered again whether Mr Ballantine knew the definition of a catamite, and I had been glad that I did. Then the memories of the journey had blurred, and I suppose I must have slept.

Now here we were. The sun was hot, the sea was warm and blue, and, on the whole, things could have been much worse. I slid back from my jumbled tatter of uncomfortable memories into the soaking, indolent heat of the present, and realized with a sudden start that a shadow had fallen across me and that somebody was speaking to me.

I sat up and blinked in the dazzle of the sun and the sunlight bouncing shrilly from the sand and sea. Somebody tall was standing a few paces from me. In the sudden glare of light, for a fraction of a second I could not tell whether this figure was black or white, male or female. I blinked again and saw a large black man, shirtless and in torn, faded trousers, white with salt, looking down at me and grinning a knowing, leering, ugly grin. I jumped hastily to my feet, clutching to me the flimsy blue of my letter to Aunt Bernice, and looked guiltily up the beach. By unspoken agreement, any communication between myself and black men was banned. It was like being on parole. Ziggy and Marsdon seemed to have seen the negro too and they were coming hastily down the beach towards us. Ziggy was running easily and fast on the hard wet sand near the sea, and Marsdon followed him stumbling and splashing in the shallows. Even at a distance I could see the rolls of fat on his ribs and shoulders wobbling. The black man caught my worried glance.

'They two your brothers?' I nodded, unwilling to explain further.

'I want speak to them.' I shrugged; Ziggy had turned away from the sea now and was coming up the beach towards us. The dry sand was very hot, and he'd tugged on a pair of battered canvas shoes to protect the soles of his feet. Marsdon had fallen behind and was half-walking, half-jogging, his shoulders and waist joggling unevenly about him.

Ziggy came up to where I stood facing the unknown negro. He would not speak to me, but the accusation in his eyes needed no words. Not another one?

'This your sister?' Ziggy nodded crossly at the man and glowered at me.

'She very beautiful.' Ziggy snarled, and then looked over his shoulder for Marsdon. Marsdon spoke Swahili, which, but for his hopeless stutter, would be fluent. He was useful at telling people to go away, despite his awkwardness.

'I have sister too. She also very beautiful.' Ziggy said nothing, but continued his angry glare, beaming it at some point between myself and this unwelcome stranger. Marsdon blundered up to us. Like Ziggy he had pulled on his shoes sloppily and he stumbled slightly over them. He was panting and gasping and his face was red and sweaty. He looked questioningly

159

at Ziggy, but Ziggy was still looking at nobody. The man grinned, a sharp, piranha grin showing a cluster of decaying teeth.

'I have two sister,' he said, and the emphasis was on two, 'both very beautiful.' He half-turned and called something sharply over his shoulder. Two girls came cautiously out on to the beach from the shade of the palms, from the direction in which Ziggy had been looking. He flushed a little and I wondered if he had been watching them.

They were both slender and lithe, and their faces had the fine, unnegroid features of Somali Arabs, with huge dark eyes and delicate, aristocratic mouths and noses. Each was wrapped in a single stretch of a diaphanous white cotton which accentuated the graceful elegance of their stride. They were exceptionally beautiful and clearly no blood relation of the man who claimed they were his sisters. They smiled shyly at us, particularly at Ziggy, then looked down at their feet, patterned with henna, rippling through the hot glinting white sand.

'You want to know my sister better?' The man was addressing Ziggy, and he had taken the hand of the slimmer of the two girls and pulled her forward a step. His voice was soft, inviting, evil. Ziggy flushed.

'No. Go away. Marsdon, tell Zag to go back to the house. Tell these people to go away.'

I turned and started walking away. I walked slowly, trailing my feet in the sand. I could hear Marsdon speaking to the man in a fumble of halting Swahili. The man's laugh rang out, coarsely and without humour. At the brow of the beach I paused and turned. Ziggy and Marsdon were following me, moving away from where the tall, ugly negro and his two 'sisters' stood in a line on the beach. His voice rang out at the backs of the two young white men.

'Hey! I think you want to know my sister better. She very nice to know. Very beautiful. We be here in the morning very early. We wait for you here tomorrow at six. All right? All right?'

Neither Ziggy nor Marsdon answered or turned. I waited for them to catch up with me, and watched the man point at Ziggy, give me a cheeky half-wave and then disappear back into the palm trees with his two female companions.

'Where do you manage to find these people, Zag?'

His voice was full of tired exasperation, but they were the first words that Ziggy had spoken to me since we had left Marsdon Villas. Strangely, the incident on the beach had allowed Ziggy to grant me some measure of forgiveness. Although I did not understand, I flushed with pleasure and delight.

I understood a little better, perhaps, the following morning. The click of the front door woke me before six, just as the sky was fading into the violet evanescence of the pre-sunrise calm. I swung out of bed, but the house was quiet with the warmth of sleep. I could hear the snuffling snores of Marsdon drifting unevenly through the shadows and I crept towards the bedroom that he and Ziggy shared. The door was ajar, and I could see Marsdon's iumpish form sprawled across his bed, hazy under the mosquito net, the sheet twisted untidily around his lower torso. Ziggy's mosquito net was bundled up into a knot, and his bed was an empty rumple of sheets. Even before I saw this, I knew that he had gone, tiptoeing from the bungalow to the beach to improve his acquaintance with somebody's sister in the soft silver light of the Indian Ocean dawn.

After that, the days at Ocean View passed in a haze of sunshine and the sea, and the days were happy ones. For perhaps the first time I felt that Ziggy was starting to see me as a person rather than as a troublesome affliction in his existence, as an equal rather than as a hopeless inferior. He began to include me in his life rather than tolerate me, and we played together, swimming side by side in the sea and wrestling with each other in the clear rippling shallows. The feelings of happy companionship which appeared and grew between the three of us flourished in the sunshine, and the traumas of Marsdon Villas seemed distant and long ago.

Even Marsdon's fumbling, bumbling stammer seemed to ease away slightly. On my birthday they gave me presents of beautiful, fantastic shells that they had bought from some unknown diver. Purloined from the cooler reaches of the Indian Ocean, I knew that when held against my ear in Cornwall I would hear in them not the rhythmic slosh of the warm waves but the echo of happy memories. My fortnightly letters to Aunt Bernice became light-hearted flutters of pale blue descriptions of a life that I knew she would disapprove, seeking always for the treachery and disaster that lurk in the depths of indolent luxury. We had agreed to return to Marsdon Villas for Christmas, but until then the days stretched ahead in a glorious golden glitter.

Despite the contented warmth that pervaded our hedonists' lifestyle, there were hidden shadows that were never mentioned. Arabella was one of these and Onyango another (although I knew without asking or being told that he had vanished from the vicinity of Marsdon Villas) and the pimp and his two 'sisters' whom we had met on the beach another. Often as we wandered after breakfast to the beach I would see the tall, ugly negro lurking amongst the palms and leering out at us, but we never commented upon him and Ziggy barely flinched. I wondered whether Marsdon had noticed Ziggy's dawn departures from Ocean View on alternate mornings, for he was always back by breakfast time, and it was, like the object of his assignations, never mentioned. I was vaguely reminded of the summer in Cornwall which seemed so

162

long ago, when, while Marsdon had snored in a graceless bundle on the beach, Ziggy, under my furtive, voyeuristic gaze, had kept his trysts with Samantha Crookshaw.

If I had been wise and cynical or, like Aunt Bernice, grumpy and querulous, I would perhaps have predicted an unhappy, abrupt ending of our tranquil seaside pleasure, but I did not. Christmas and the insecurity of my return to Marsdon Villas were far enough away that I lived only in the present and basked in its happiness. The day to day existence of unhurried leisure, feasting on freshly-caught fish and freshly-picked fruit, swimming, playing, laughing and sleeping on the sand, sustained me and warmed me and I looked no further.

Late afternoon and the sun was still bright in the hot blue of the sky, when Ziggy joggled me awake with his suntanned elbow. Marsdon lay face down in the sand beside him. As on those distant Cornish beaches, Marsdon's mouth drooped open and a trail of saliva drooled from the corner of his lips. There was a damp stain on his shirt into which his podgy face was scrunched. Whereas Ziggy had tanned to a rich metallic bronze, Marsdon had burnt and peeled and burnt again. His shoulders looked raw and painful. I watched as Ziggy carefully draped his own shirt across Marsdon's back to protect him a little from the burning rays of the end-of-the-day sun. Marsdon twitched and snorted a little as the solicitously-placed shirt touched his skin, bunching his own shirt in his fist like a small child, but he did not wake up.

Ziggy smiled and jerked his head away from Marsdon, and began to walk further up the beach. I stood up slowly and cautiously, careful not to spray sand over the fat body at my feet, and followed.

For a while we sat in silence, looking eastwards out

over the blue calmness. I wondered how many times Ziggy had seen the sun rise over the Indian Ocean, but for all our developing friendship I was too shy to ask him. It would be infringing on one of the taboo subjects. Ziggy spoke suddenly, abruptly, awkwardly, his voice harsh. He was looking down at his feet which were kicking a trench in the soft sand.

'Zag, do you have any money with you?' I was surprised, and answered without thinking.

'What, here? On the beach?'

'No.' His voice was irritated, but I also could detect shame and panic in his voice. Strange emotions, surely, for my glorious golden brother.

'In the bungalow? Well, I have some. Not much. Why don't you ask Marsdon? Max sends him some every week, you know. For food and the house servant and stuff.'

I had purposefully distanced myself from the house servant, to such an extent that I didn't even know the name of the neat quiet elderly lady who cooked and cleaned for us.

'How much money do you have?'

I looked hard at Ziggy then, but he continued to look away, no longer staring at his feet, but gazing straight out across the sea. His face in profile was very handsome, but also seemed very hard, and there was something else in his expression too that I could not at first place. Then I saw it: fear. My wonderful, heroic Ziggy was afraid. My voice was quick with anxiety.

'I told you, not much. I'm not sure of the amount. Why don't you ask Marsdon?' He met my eyes then, in a brief flicker of a glance that had passed before I had even registered it.

'Because.'

'Because?'

'Yes. Because.'

How slow and foolish could I be? Slow and foolish enough for the question which puzzled me not to be

164

'why does he want money?' but 'why can't he ask Marsdon?' Then, suddenly, in that strange way for which there seems to be no logical explanation, I understood.

'It's for . . . ?' I knew no names and as my voice tailed away in the heat my question evaporated, but already Ziggy had nodded in reply.

'How much does he want?' Even as I asked I knew that it would be the tall ugly pimp demanding cash rather than the beautiful young Somali girl. Ziggy shrugged irritably, but I knew now that his exasperation was a product of nervous fear.

'Enough. He says that she's pregnant.'

How quiet can silence be? It went on and on, out-burning the heat of the afternoon sun, out-glaring the sparkle of the sea and the white glittering of the sand. Stretching onwards and forever, until with a twitch and a liquid, slobbering grunt, a little further down the beach it woke Marsdon up.

Chapter Eleven

Ocean View, Malindi, Kenya.
Dear Aunt Bernice,
I expect that you are finding it strange receiving this letter so soon after my last one.
I am writing this on behalf of Ziggy as he is too ashamed to write to you himself. Unfortunately he has run into a terrible problem concerning a girl here and he is in desperate need of money to settle things. We turn to you as the guardian that our father chose for us to beg for your help. We feel that we should not bother Marsdon and his family with Ziggy's problems.
If you could help him in this sad plight we will realize again the kindness and wisdom of our father's choice. Ziggy says that he will repay you out of his next allowance. Fifty pounds should be enough. At this terrible time I include you in my prayers more frequently than ever. Yours lovingly, Zag. PS Please reply quickly.

I reread the letter, added in a few missing commas and a few commas that should have remained missing, blew the glittering speckles of white sand out of the fold and handed it across Marsdon's recumbent, snoring form to Ziggy. I felt rather proud of my composition. Revealing, but not too revealing, and appealing to the wrinkled vanity of Aunt Bernice's pocket. I knew that despite her meagre style of living she had plenty of available money. The difficulty was tempting her to part with it. She had never apparently taken to heart the old adage of being unable to take it with you. Ziggy read the letter quickly. I could follow the jerking darts of his eyes down the page. He grunted.

'Well. Don't you like it?'

'I don't see why you have to mention the girl.'

'I don't.'

'Yes you do.'

'I don't say that she's black or a prostitute or possibly pregnant, but I have to say something. If I asked her for money with no reason she'd suspect terrible things, even worse things than the truth, and she'd never send it.' Another grunt.

'Well, you know that's true. Is something else wrong?'

'All this stuff about our father, well it's a bit . . . I don't know, overstated, isn't it? I'm worried about how she'll take it as well. She's getting old, you know. I mean she was old enough when you were a baby, so she's positively ancient now. You know that I told Max that the old bat shouldn't hear about your little . . . well, you know, with Onyango.'

Oh, how the barriers, years in the building, between myself and Ziggy were tumbling down around us. I shared a secret with him, I squabbled with him, he called Aunt Bernice 'the old bat' and now he'd broken yet more taboos by mentioning Onyango. Perhaps I'd tell him all about Onyango one day. I felt ridiculously, selfishly pleased with life.

'She'll like all that stuff about our father, it will appeal to her vanity. It's probably the only thing that will persuade her to send you any money. You know what she's like. Anyway, she probably expects this sort of thing from you, being male and things. It was only ever me that had to stay at home and keep quiet and be good. It's one of the penalties of being a girl. She's probably surprised you haven't done it before. Anyway, if you don't like it you can write it yourself.'

Marsdon took the letter to be posted the next morning.

167

He did not question my request for urgency and I wondered, not for the first time, what thoughts went on behind the bewildered and ugly face that masked his mind. There had been no secret dawn departure and rendezvous for Ziggy that morning and he looked tired. When he pleaded a headache and said he was going to stay inside, again Marsdon asked no questions.

I walked down to the beach with Marsdon, and the menacing black shadow of the pimp lurked amongst the ribbed trunks of the palms and leered at us. I was afraid that he would accost us and reveal Ziggy's secret in front of Marsdon, but I realized that my fear was one born of selfishness; I did not want Ziggy to have anybody else to share his problems with. Being sole confidante to Ziggy gave me power in a relationship that I had coveted since I could remember.

How short-lived was that power. In ten days' time it shrivelled in the noonday heat with the arrival of a mustard-yellow envelope. It was the second telegram I had seen. The first had been almost exactly three years earlier and announced the death in London of Aunt Bernice's sister, Eveline. This telegram also went, straight and callous, to the point; telegrams always do. Aunt Bernice had collapsed in the chill of her kitchen, she had been found surprisingly quickly by the coalman a few hours later and she had died in hospital within the day. A last request, no doubt snarled to the efficient calm of the attendant nurse, was a sad plea for there to be a minimum of three mourners at her funeral. She wanted one more mourner than Eveline.

It was not astounding how two of the potential mourners had been tracked down so rapidly. She had collapsed clutching a letter which she had just opened. Our address at Ocean View had headed the paper.

The funeral in the little grey churchyard on the headland overlooking the bay was a curious affair.

Perhaps funerals always are, especially those of the unloved. The weather was as grey and damply soft as a pigeon's breast and there was not a breath of wind. Ziggy and I stood opposite each other on either side of the grave. The turned earth smelt deliciously rich and there were earthworms, some severed in half by the sexton's spade, wriggling in the loamy pile. Our suntanned faces seemed both ridiculous and cheekily inappropriate.

My mother, the third mourner, teetered and cackled at the head of the grave, where the stone would soon be erected, with a brisk efficient Bodwell nurse on either side of her, supporting her and restraining her. The starched white uniforms of the nurses seemed likewise ridiculous and inappropriate. The pinched grey faces, the drab dark clothes of death and the resigned sobriety that Aunt Bernice would have wanted, that even her sister, half-chewed Eveline, had managed, had eluded her. The sullen yews that stood in silent sentry amongst the granite gravestones would have pleased her more as mourners, and they creaked and groaned despite the absence of the slightest breeze. Even in death Aunt Bernice was wronged, and she was not there to indulge in feeling bitter.

All the same, she had flowers which Eveline had not. A huge, gaudy wreath selected by the Bodwell nurses on behalf of my mother and an even bigger, gaudier wreath that somehow Marsdon's family and the Hannetts had managed to have delivered at the right time to the right place straddled the cheap plain coffin. Between the wreaths rested a bunch of drooping flowers, irises and freesias, that in comparison to the other two offerings looked both squalid and stingy, as though stolen from a funeral of several days ago. It was from Ziggy and me.

So much of my life had been shaped and moulded by Aunt Bernice. I had spent so many silent, rancid hours with her, eating, reading, even praying, and yet in the pearly fogginess of her funeral I could feel no emotion at all. No grief, no joy, no relief, and the vicar's carefully selected words, brief and bland, seemed to me to be as empty and devoid of meaning as my mother's insane ramblings that accompanied him.

I looked up at Ziggy and his handsome sun-bronzed face stared back at me with cold eyes. It was like looking at an unfriendly stranger. He was convinced that it was my letter of which I was so proud that had felled Aunt Bernice, and I was guiltily afraid, despite kindly reassurances from the hospital where she died, that he was right. Although Ziggy had not said as much, I knew that Aunt Bernice's death had wakened in him again the cataloguing of disasters that I seemed to have a propensity for, and I knew that he derided, feared and resented me for my apparent engendering of catastrophes.

Tears welled in my eyes, and one dribbled unhurriedly down my tanned cheek. The vicar patted my shoulder kindly and one of my mother's efficient nurses handed me a clean, crisply folded handkerchief. I dabbed at my eyes forlornly, and I knew that the saddest, baddest thing was that my tears were not for Aunt Bernice but for the loss of Ziggy's confidence and friendship.

As we edged through the grey stone arch of the entrance to the churchyard, inscribed with some mystical words in Cornish, I could hear the thump of the clods of earth being thrown back in over Aunt Bernice. It was a strange sound to hear. We kissed our mother on her pale mauve-powdered cheek that smelt of stale sugared almonds, first Ziggy and then me, and she was whisked away by her brisk efficient nurses, back to the sterile warmth of Bodwell. Ziggy and I were left standing alone outside the graveyard, a black and white collie from one of the nearby farms fawning around our feet.

Back at Aunt Bernice's tall narrow house, the house

of my childhood, the white gate, still ajar, creaked on its hinges and the small windows were dirty and impassive in their stare. The atmosphere of the house was that of death: cold and clammy, dark and dusty. We both shivered. The large ungainly furniture seemed to have grown and cluttered the narrow rooms of the house even more than I remembered, creating shadows within shadows, gloom within gloom.

We went into the kitchen and I made a pot of tea. The tea leaves in the old metal caddy smelt of mould and clung together damply in mossy clumps, but I boiled the kettle anyway and poured a mug of tea for each of us. We were waiting for the lawyer to arrive, and we sat in silence, sipping our mildewed tea, listening to the endless echo of death, and breathing in the pervasive dank aroma of cessation and decay. I could feel myself tumbling helplessly down the abyss of time into my lonely, lost years of childhood.

Struggling to escape I stood up abruptly, clattering my chipped white china mug down so sharply that the unfinished dregs of fusty tea slopped and splashed on to the table.

'It's oppressive in here. I'm going outside.'

I felt as though I was suffocating in the dismal murk of the house and I hurried to the front door as frantically as in a nightmare. I thudded off the arm of one of the huge leather armchairs, button-backed and solid with horsehair, and barked my shins on one of the half-opened drawers of the heavy wooden sideboard.

I stood on the lank winter grass of the front lawn and breathed deeply, taking in huge gulps of the soft, wet, salty air as though it were a life-restoring draught after severe thirst. A short round man in a suit so dark that it looked almost green, rolled through the dangling gate and minced up the drive towards me. He had steel-rimmed spectacles perched on his nose, a black briefcase, an insincere smile and a completely bald

171

head that gleamed as though polished or wet in the sunless, grey afternoon. Everything about him screamed of bureaucracy and petty officiousness; he was clearly the awaited lawyer. I accosted him before he drew level with me.

'Hello. You must be Mr Rowe. My brother is waiting for you inside. I'm afraid that I don't feel well so I'll be staying out here in the garden for a while.'

The smile slid from Mr Rowe's sleek cheeks.

'I was very sorry to hear about the death of Miss . . . errr . . . your aunt, your guardian, I mean.'

I felt reproved. It was clearly etiquette to honour and dismiss the deceased with some suitably trite, if false, remarks before getting down to business.

'Yes. I suppose that she was old. Everybody seems to keep saying that anyway.'

The synthetic smile slimed again across his smooth round face without reaching his pebble eyes. I was learning.

'A heart attack, I understand.'

'Yes.'

'Well, as you say, she had a good long life.'

His unctuous insincerity grated across me. I had fled the claustrophobia of the house only to be swaddled in the sycophancy of Mr Rowe's smug mendacity.

'I said that she was old. There is a subtle difference.'

A discreet pause with the smile erased, and then a cold

'I see.'

Another discreet pause and the smile struggled to realign itself.

'I was hoping to see you rather than your brother. You did live with the deceased, your guardian, while your brother was away at school.'

I shrugged irritably. I wanted this servile Mr Rowe to slide out of my sight. I didn't want to hear any more of his slick, false, toadying words dripping, cloying and glutinous, from his lawyer tongue. If childhood threats were true, I thought, then his tongue would surely be covered in pimples. My interest in him briefly aroused, I peered forward to try and peek inside his mouth. I couldn't see, of course, and I rocked backwards again on my heels.

'I'll come inside shortly. I just want a breath of fresh air.'

I jerked my head dismissively in the direction of the front door and walked deliberately past Mr Rowe towards the garden gate. He hesitated behind me, then as I heard his shiny black shoes crunch into the gravel as he headed towards the front door, I paused, turned and gazed after his stout, flouncing back. He was not completely bald as I had initially thought; some straggling wisps of grey hair were smeared down the back of his bald head. They looked self-conscious and diffident and for just a lingering second I felt ashamed that I had sent him in alone to face the gloom and cheerless shadows of my childhood home. The clumsy furniture would rise in an awkard damp huddle to meet and obstruct him and Ziggy would pour him an ugly mugful of mouldy tea.

I shrugged again and walked onwards down the garden towards the front gate. The yellowed straggly grass was rank and wet and I kicked up a fine spray of water that darkened the toes of my shoes. The clumps of bamboo straggled and fretted timelessly in front of the garden wall. I pushed behind them, and trampling unthinkingly the shallow graves of crab claws from a sad, resentful summer that seemed a hundred years ago, I scrambled on to the wall and looked out over the sea. The horizon was a cloudy smudge where the lead-grey sky blurred into the lead-grey sea. The sea was an endless mass of water and the huge, close sky seemed heavy with water too, but I felt as dry as the shrivelled, parchment skin of a long-dead desiccated gecko in the Kenyan sun.

I wondered how often I'd sat, cold-bottomed, on the

wall, kicking my awkward, petulant heels against the granite blocks and letting my mind drift without direction, from the starting point of the sea to a thousand million other aimless, pointless thoughts. But did I really have such a variety of thoughts? So many times in my schoolday evenings I had dreamed of Ziggy, somewhere else, in some other life, so unknown and so distant. Often I had idly fantasized a fairytale return, with Aunt Bernice suddenly away, or for her absence to be permanent, dead. Then we had lived together, happily ever after, just Ziggy and myself, with nobody else there to interrupt our contented, intimate companionship. I paused suddenly in my web of thoughts of my thoughts, aghast at their morbid aptness and greedy, gruesome pertinence. But the dream was still a dream, I still sat on the wall, alone and lonely, looking out over the indifferent sea.

It was beginning to rain. Small speckles of drizzle fluttered sideways into my eyes and hair. I recalled that I had once all but worshipped the sea, offering up a litany of prayers and promises. How long ago that seemed. Tears welled in my eyes at the memories, and just a few spilled and wandered slowly down my cheeks. Reminiscences and realization of loss of even an empty childhood can still be forlorn and sad. In those few straggling tears spilt for memories of my past I mourned for Aunt Bernice, but I knew that her era had ended even before her death. In my heart I called out to that sea god of my childhood to realize that like the claws of the tortured crabs behind me, Aunt Bernice too was dead and buried.

There was a scuffle in the bamboo which could not be the wind rustling the fronds, for the humid air was completely still. I jumped around guiltily, worried that I might have inadvertently spoken aloud my supplication to the sea. It was Ziggy. His face seemed thin and rather hard, but his expression softened a little as he looked at my startled face. The tears had not yet dried on my cheeks, and I suppose he might have thought that I had been truly mourning and weeping for Aunt Bernice.

'Mr Rowe is waiting to see you inside. I gave him a cup of that horrible tea you made.'

'Why does he want to see me? Can't he just see you?'

'It's about the will.'

'The will?' I had not thought of wills nor any of the practicalities that come hand-in-hand with death. This narrow ugly house had always been my home, this hard cold granite wall behind the bamboos had always been my haven. I had, naively, unthinkingly, assumed that it always would be. Ziggy's face seemed stiff and unsmiling, and his incongruous tan appeared a sickly ochre in this pale, livid light. I was suddenly afraid.

'The will?' I repeated, and then 'why me?'

I could heard the tremor of fear squeaking sharply through my voice.

'There's no need for you to get so upset. She's left you everything.'

Just like that I was rich. Strangely, suddenly, under the cold obsequious eyes of Mr Rowe I gathered to myself my inherited wealth. Aunt Bernice had left nothing for Ziggy, in fact nothing for anybody but myself. Ziggy still had his allowance from my father's estate which he would receive until my mother died and my parents' property was divided between us, but I was already rich.

For two hours, maybe more, Mr Rowe stayed with me in the chill dark kitchen, my chill dark kitchen, completing the business of unexpected inheritance. He explained in tedious detail clauses and investments, title deeds and transfers. I signed where he told me to sign, with my gawky adolescent signature, but his words slid in their obsequious slime around me. The only thing that I knew was that I was rich, that Aunt Bernice had suddenly played her trump card of stacked wealth, but whether it was for the years that I had lived in silent bitterness with her or whether it was a gesture on the behalf of the repressed, sad childhoods that we had both, like sisters, survived, I would never be able to decide.

Ziggy sulked at my unexpected affluence. I suppose that it seemed like another episode in the series of my spoiling his chances.

'What do you want money for?' he asked gruffly and querulously in the evening after Mr Rowe had gone. I had lit a fire in the kitchen and was standing at the stove grilling a pair of mackerel. The dark blue and stark white skins gleamed and then dulled in the heat as they rose in blisters, bursting to brown scars and dripping trails of fish oil. Ziggy was slouched at the wooden table, slumped forward on his chair with his head propped on his arms.

'I don't. I just don't want not to have money. I don't want to have to be dependent on you or anyone else.' A pause and then I added, 'Anyway, now you can always ask me for money if you're afraid you have got somebody pregnant.'

I was trying to lighten the sullen shrouds of darkness that seemed draped between us. With the sudden commotion of Aunt Bernice's death we had managed to skate away from Ocean View without giving the ugly negro pimp any money at all.

I held the mackerel carefully in the tips of my fingers by the ends of their charred, crumbling tails. I flipped them over, one by one. Ziggy scratched his chair away from the table and towards the fire. The house was still ponderous with cold and our beds were going to feel damp later.

'What about this?' He gestured behind him vaguely, with a wave of both his arms. He did not turn round, but glowered into the fire. It was a smoky, sulky fire that seemed to be cowering away from the chill of the room.

'What?' I left the mackerel briefly and poked the fire. It spluttered a little, unwilling to be coaxed into life, but a few licks of flame crackled grudgingly at the coals.

'The house.'

To me it wasn't 'the house', it was home. Even if my days of growing up here had not been very happy, dogged by chilly beds, querulous fires and stilted conversations, I still did not want to cut my umbilical cord to the past just yet. I could hear the wind rising outside, and I knew that the garden wall stood, silent and solid, behind the unheard, rhythmic susurration of the bamboo.

'Oh. The house. I'll keep it. I've got to live somewhere and so have you until you decide what you want to do.'

'But what about all her stuff? There's piles of it and it's all horrible.'

'We could sort it out. We both could. Couldn't we?' I slid the mackerel on to the plates. I was pleading for friendship now, and I held one plate out to Ziggy like a peace offering. He took it from me, and swung around from the fire to sit at the table.

'I suppose so,' he conceded grudgingly, 'but I'm not staying in poky old Cornwall for ever.'

It was enough and I slumped into my chair with relief. If I had been completely condemned for my sudden wealth he would be leaving tomorrow. If I was careful and lucky, in the days ahead of rooting through Aunt Bernice's possessions and renovating the house I might be able to coax our hours of Ocean View comradeship to life again, even in the rainy chill of British weather.

I smiled hopefully, encouragingly across the table at Ziggy. He was chewing on the succulent oily flesh of the mackerel and withdrawing the long bones of the ribcage between his teeth. The fire, brighter now, gleamed on his oily fingers. He met my smile with a brief flicker of acknowledgement in his eyes.

* * *

It was only days until Christmas and the house seemed huge, emptied now of its ponderous furniture, when the third telegram of my life crunched up the gravel drive and was flipped nonchalantly into my hands. It was for Ziggy and it was from Kenya. I took it upstairs to where Ziggy stood on a stepladder painting the ceiling of his room. I guessed it was going to be an inane Christmas greeting.

Disasters here stop Please come stop Mr and Mrs Hannett murdered stop Arabella devastated stop Expect you before Christmas stop Please send arrival times stop Marsdon stop

Chapter Twelve

It was the middle of January before Ziggy and I were able to reach Kenya, and finally stand, silent and solemn, before the second grave in the shade of the euphorbia hedge in the grounds of Max's tiny white-washed church. Although the funeral had been nearly two months ago the earth of the grave still looked raw and scarred, and it was too early yet for a stone to have been set. We had bought flowers in the market in Kericho, great bundles of flamboyant tropical blooms that would have dwarfed our floral offering at Aunt Bernice's funeral shamefully. I laid the flowers gently across the dry earth mound, placing them carefully and quietly as though I might disturb some delicate thing if I was rough or clumsy. As we stood and contemplated the grave I watched the flowers succumb to the sun's heat, drooping first, and then becoming limp and lifeless under the creeping fingers of plasmolysis.

We stood, side by side, for perhaps ten minutes, maybe more, by the Hannetts' grave. Ziggy held himself perfectly upright, stiff and motionless. His steady gaze, fixed on some point at the grave-head where the stone would one day stand with names and dates and perhaps some trite epitaph, was inward and remote. I wondered what he could be thinking about behind that rigid exterior. A few paces behind us I could hear Marsdon's uneven, snuffling breathing as he restlessly shifted from one foot to the other.

My eyes flicked between the wilting flowers, to Ziggy's withdrawn face, to the red dusty track where the car and driver waited for us. I knew that the mourning rituals of the Kalenjin people were loud and dramatic, and I wondered too what he was thinking of our stiff silence. I found it hard to contemplate death and mourning under the huge expanse of a summer-blue, bright sky.

Ziggy sighed, relaxed his stiff square-shouldered posture a little, and turned his head towards me.

'Have you finished paying your respects?'

I nodded, unsure that I had even started or knew how to. I had really not been thinking of the Hannetts at all as we stood beside their grave. I had wondered why and how and when they had died of course, and whether they had truly been murdered, but I had wondered that many times already. I had wondered about what Arabella would do now, and whether she had turned to the desirable Mr Ballantine for solace, and whether he had accepted her. I had briefly tried to imagine the grimness and tropical heat of the Hannetts' funeral, but I had not really thought about the Hannetts themselves. I had known them briefly, superficially for a few weeks in which they had despised me and pitied me, and I, in a smug, bitter, ugly way, had despised and pitied them. In life they had seemed no less distant than now, with their bodies, probably fast decaying in the hungry tropical soil, buried under the ground at my feet.

Marsdon coughed softly, anxiously at our backs and we turned to go. I looked up at Ziggy's face, but his expression remained an unreadable mask. I wondered again what he had been thinking of in those long hot minutes of graveside silence. If he had been praying, for whom or for what? Apart from his infatuation with Arabella, I could not see that Ziggy was any closer to the Hannetts than I. In fact, I probably knew them better than he did.

We headed away from the graves. Marsdon was walking a little in front of us, and he led the way not back to the track and the car, but to the cool interior of the church. We followed without questioning him.

Inside the church Jacob, or Jacob-the-catamite as I always thought of him now, was polishing the wooden benches and pews. He was on his knees beside them on the cool stone floor, a torn white rag in one hand and a bar of yellow wax in the other. The smoky-clean smell of polish mingled pleasingly with the other scent of the church that I remembered: the summertime, Cornish hedgerow smell of salt and fennel. As we approached him, Jacob turned to us, his huge liquid doe eyes framing a question. The opening of the church door as we entered had brought a brief glare of afternoon light which was cut off sharply as the door swung closed behind us. Jacob did not stand up but stayed kneeling, as though in deference, at our feet. The upturned soles of his feet were pink and looked strangely vulnerable.

'Where,' asked Marsdon, 'is Father Mannering?'

In answer, Jacob turned his gazelle-eyed gaze towards the altar. Father Mannering was on his knees beside the altar table, his face buried in his hands. So close was he to the altar that the white cloth which covered it trailed into his own robes.

'He is praying,' explained Jacob in a reverential whisper, as though it might not be obvious to us. I wondered what Father Mannering might pray for; for himself, for Jacob, for his congregation who scorned him, or for his sins.

Marsdon looked uncomfortable. He glanced quickly from his crunched-up, piggy eyes between Ziggy, Father Mannering and me, and then back to Jacob who still knelt before us. It was clear that Marsdon had hoped to speak to Father Mannering but had not expected to have to interrupt him at prayer. I was irritated by Marsdon's lingering hesitancy. I was tired and wanted to return to Marsdon Villas. Marsdon had met us at the front door as soon as we had arrived. He had immediately taken our bags from us, given them to a handy servant and whisked us out of the house to the church. We had not spoken to Max or Lily or Arabella or even seen them, nor had we unpacked, rested or washed. I tutted crossly, and Ziggy seemed to be feeling likewise, for he jabbed Marsdon in his pudgy waist with his elbow.

'Come on, Marsdon,' he muttered. 'What do you want to see old Mannering for? I've said all the prayers I wanted to say outside.'

Ziggy's irritated nudge seemed to goad Marsdon into action. He coughed loudly and deliberately, and the cool quietness of the church was splintered by the ugly, awkward noise. Father Mannering clambered to his feet with an uneven stiffness as though he had been kneeling for a long time. He turned to face us.

'Can I help you?' he called.

Marsdon went up to where Father Mannering stood at the altar and spoke to him. We could hear him stammering out an anxious message to the vicar disturbed from his altar-side prayers without apology. Marsdon's voice was subdued and the words indistinguishable, but the jerky rhythm of his voice was parodied mockingly by the church's cavernous echo. Father Mannering nodded as his message spluttered gracelessly to its end, then turned away from Marsdon's anxious red face.

'Jacob,' called Father Mannering, and the beautiful negro boy sprang nimbly up, and ran on his bare feet to Father Mannering. Together they left the church, Father Mannering first, with his forgettable, vague face staring vacantly downwards, and Jacob following close behind him, still clutching his cake of wax and his polishing rag of surrender. The three of us were left alone in the suddenly silent, dim coolness.

Marsdon walked back to where we stood. His face was still flushed and he was breathing awkwardly, almost panting as though he had been running.

'I had to speak to you before we went back to the house,' he said quickly. His stuttered words rattled and tumbled over each other like clattering round stones in a fast-flowing river.

'There's so many things you ought to know, and this was the only place I could think of telling you in private.'

He paused, and took a deep, sucking breath between his buck teeth. I assumed that he was going to tell us some details of the Hannetts' death, and I felt the excitement of morbid curiosity rising irresistibly inside me. I glanced sideways at Ziggy. He had sat down in a pew and his expression seemed weary, withdrawn and indifferent. I was ashamed then of my vulture-like eagerness for gory description, and I sat down next to him subdued.

There was a pause, and then Marsdon turned to me, his face red and puffy and his eyes bulging with angry, unshed tears.

'What did you have to come back for anyway?' he asked. But for his stammer his voice would have been vicious, but his speech impediment tripped up his venom as effectively as it tripped up his words. 'Haven't you caused enough trouble here already?'

I was surprised and shocked, but perhaps more by his bold, furious tone than by his words. I gaped at him wordlessly, and it was Ziggy who answered for me.

'That's in the past, Marsdon. You know it is. It's over. Zag paid for me to come back here, you know. You asked me to come. I couldn't have just left her in Cornwall on her own. She paid for both of us. Aren't there more important things that have happened now, and can't we forget the past?'

Marsdon nodded and muttered something that I couldn't catch. Then he shook his head as though clearing something out of his tussocks of fusty hair. He seemed to have surprised himself by his own outburst, but he did not appear to be convinced by Ziggy's reply.

Marsdon began to rummage nervously in his pockets. He soon brought out of one of them a piece of paper torn roughly from a notebook. It was a grubby scrap of paper, folded irregularly, smeared and greasily grey. He sat down on the bench in front of the pew on which Ziggy and I were perched, and turning to face us, unfolded the paper on his lap. I could see an untidy list disjointedly scrawled in pencil.

'I've just written a few things down so that I don't leave anything out,' he told us. Despite the tattiness of the paper it seemed a remarkably organized idea for Marsdon. He blushed as he looked at his notes. As he began to stammer out his uncomfortable, awkward list he stared fixedly at it, not once looking up and meeting either Ziggy's or my eyes.

'First of all, Ziggy owes me about twenty-five pounds. That man on the beach with a couple of sisters demanded it. I ignored him at first but he seemed able to provide proof of his story, so I paid out of some of the money sent down for food.'

I felt Ziggy squirm uneasily on the pew beside me, but Marsdon, perhaps almost as uncomfortable as Ziggy, moved quickly on to his next point. His stammer and the gabbling speed at which he was relating his list made him difficult to understand.

'Secondly, Mr Ballantine has stopped working for us. He is actually leaving Marsdon Villas today so you won't be seeing him. Thirdly, about the Hannetts. I feel you should briefly know the circumstances of their horrible deaths so that you don't . . .'

The door of the church had swung open again, and we all looked up towards the white rectangle of bright afternoon light. As the door closed, the silhouette that had opened it gained features. It was Arabella.

All three of us stood up, hastily, guiltily. Marsdon stuffed his scrap of paper into his pocket, and wiped his sweaty palms on the seat of his shorts. She came towards where we stood like a band of startled conspirators and her delicate eyebrows were raised into arches of surprise. Her whole bearing seemed more beautiful and more haughty than ever, despite the grief of the past months.

'Ziggy! I didn't realize you had arrived so soon. How nice to see you! And funny little Zag too.'

There was a self-assured pleasure in her voice, and out of the corner of my eye I could see Ziggy responding to her presence. Unconsciously, he was straightening his back to match her height, consciously he was smiling with delight and reaching out his hands to take hers. His condolences were bathed in such sincerity, subdued smiles and gravity of such correct proportions that I felt sure he must have been practising or taking lessons in etiquette. With shame I realized that my feelings were not of empathy for Arabella's bereavement, nor even of hurt at being 'funny little Zag', but the tight clutch of jealousy and possessive fear as I watched again Ziggy being taken away from me so easily and so completely. Arabella turned to Marsdon.

'Why didn't you tell me they had arrived? You know how much I was longing to see Ziggy again. I would have liked to have been the one to show him where dear Mummy and Daddy lie.'

The bitter knot of exclusion tightened and burned inside me, but also I was surprised. Previously Ziggy had doted upon Arabella and she had all but ignored him, much preferring to seek favour with Mr Ballantine. Perhaps Mr Ballantine's sudden and unexplained departure from Marsdon Villas had caused him to tumble from the position of elevation that he had previously held in Arabella's eyes. Or perhaps he had committed a great sin, although that seemed improbable, which had precipitated both his departure and his fall from grace. I did not ponder on these ideas then, they merely flickered into my mind and then out again, leaving a yawning gap of jealousy.

Ziggy and Arabella were walking slowly together

towards the door of the church, arm in arm, Marsdon and I trailing a little way behind them. With a sudden flash of foreboding and premonition I felt as though we were the bridesmaid and best man following the newly-wed, happy couple. I could feel the ache of loneliness and rancour thudding inside me.

There were two cars glinting on the dirt road beside the church now, and the negro drivers of both were unloading flowers from the car that Arabella had arrived in and piling them on her parents' grave.

'I bring a carload of flowers every week,' I could hear Arabella's beautiful, singing voice explaining to Ziggy. 'Of course, I didn't realize that you had so kindly brought them some too. Their grave looks so naked, especially next to your poor father's. His looks as though it has been there forever.'

The flowers that Ziggy and I had brought were now lost under the deluge of new blossoms that were heaped high on the Hannetts' grave to wilt slowly in the sun as ours had done. Although it was true that our father's grave looked old and settled beside the Hannetts', it was not a positive comparison. Rather it looked neglected and forgotten, like the grave of a slave alongside that of an emperor. I thought of my father's gloves that I had not looked at for years and wished that I had brought them with me as a talisman of hope. They were in the misty distance of Cornwall, rolled up in their tobacco tin.

Afternoon tea at Marsdon Villas: there was the same cold, tinkling clink of fine English china, and the same cold, tinkling clink of fine English conversation. Max and Lily greeted both Ziggy and me with cordial English pleasantries, and although they displayed more pleasure at seeing Ziggy than me, that was not unusual either. I felt that they had chosen to wipe my incomprehensible, sinful behaviour from their memories, and I was glad.

Dr Cairns was there too, sour and silent as usual, and his earnest pair of medical students, Richard and Andrew, completely identical and yet completely different, peered out at life from their gooseberry eyes over their sharp avian noses with their unchanged cold scientific curiosity. The Frobishers were there too, for they had driven Ziggy and me to Marsdon Villas from Nairobi, and their conversation seemed not to have changed at all over the passing months, for it was as superior, inane and immemorable as ever. Even the two houseboys in their crisp clean uniforms, pouring the tea too slowly for Lily's liking and responding with a calm polite servitude and an unfathomable deepness in their brown-eyed gazes to her querulous snaps, seemed the same.

The sky was an abyssal, sonorous blue and the garden was draped in the tropical luxuriance of birdsong and the sweet, heavy redolence of flowers and sunshine. Amongst this, Arabella swayed and fluttered like a glorious honey-scented blossom, delicate and beautiful in our midst, while Ziggy and Marsdon, the one almost deific in his golden handsomeness and confidence and the other stumbling, awkward and flabbily gauche, trod carefully and humbly about her.

Yes, everything seemed totally unchanged, and yet there was a huge, yawning gap that screamed to be filled, and it was not the Hannetts whose absence I noticed. It was the lack of the tired smile, the kindly slanting blue eyes and the gentle, almost refined, murmur of Edinburgh that screamed out at me. But nobody mentioned that Mr Ballantine was leaving Marsdon Villas that day, in fact nobody mentioned his name at all. It seemed to be an occasion of questions that not only went unanswered, but also went unasked.

Not everything went unanswered, however. Max cleared his throat and coughed in such a manner, more

187

deliberate than loud, that the clink of chatter and china paused in the heat of the afternoon sun and turned towards him.

'I know that this is painful for all of us,' he began, booming his words out in his theatrical voice of command, 'and especially to Arabella.' At this point, without moving his stoutly planted feet, he seemed to twist his broad torso and bob in her direction. Arabella was sitting in one of the white wicker chairs and she clasped her beautiful slender hands together in her lap and looked demurely downwards at them. We all half turned towards her, and this lowering of the head seemed almost, to my critical and cynical eye, an acceptance of applause. Like the audience that I believed I perceived us to be, we all turned back again to Max as he continued.

'I think, however, that I should announce this so that we can all know and support each other. By good fortune and hard work the criminal, that animal, that perpetrated that unutterably vile monstrosity against our dear friends, Mr and Mrs Hannett, was apprehended yesterday evening in Nairobi.'

He had relished the words in his mouth as he had spoken them, spitting the words like 'criminal' and 'animal' out at us like grape pips, and rolling 'monstrosity' around in his mouth like a repugnant golf ball. If he had not been so successful in the tea industry, he might have done equally well as a politician.

At the end of his announcement there had been a communal gasp from the audience, especially from Lily. Out of the corner of my eye I could see the Frobishers, like Arabella perched on the white wicker chairs, nodding their heads wisely. They had doubtless brought this news with Ziggy and me in their car from Nairobi.

Arabella sat forward in her chair, her head raised now. She held her body very upright and she looked Max full in the face. Ziggy had moved his chair round to be next to hers, and I saw him take one of her hands in his own reassuringly. I felt the twists of envy coiling inside me, and my first thoughts that Max had been insensitive to tell Arabella this news so publicly were crushed inside me. Arabella's face seemed pale, and her huge eyes very bright, and I felt again as though I were watching a theatrical tragedy, and that Arabella might even be enjoying playing the part of the beautiful maiden in distress. It was a role in which she was very aptly cast, but it is shameful that these sardonic thoughts cruelly overrode any feelings of sympathy that I might have nurtured.

'And was it . . . ?' she breathed in a tiny, tremulous voice that seemed to call out for masculine protection. Her words, although quietly spoken, seemed to hang almost visibly like a haze in the afternoon heat. The orator in Max climbed to new heights as his voice boomed forth across the auditorium, punching into the air and into us.

'Indeed, my dear child. It seems that there can be no doubt. It was Onyango. The machete with which he hacked your beloved parents to death was still in his possession.'

Arabella fell forward with a minute, pleading sound fluttering from her lips. While Ziggy, Marsdon, Max, Lily, the Frobishers, Dr Cairns and his students, and even the house servants flapped and twittered around her fragile form, elegantly crumpled, lying unconscious on the grass, I ran, without knowing that I ran. Once around the corner of the house, alone and unwatched, I slumped on to the ground, and supported by the wall I knelt on the grass and was inelegantly and repeatedly sick, while helpless, useless tears flooded down my face.

How long was I there, kneeling by the side of the house, my head pressed against the wall and my face clawed between my hands? Even now I have no idea. Time passed slowly, and my aching body retched and groaned and retched again, as though trying to eject with the foul, sweeping waves of nausea the horror of my thoughts and knowledge. When I finally stood up my legs felt unsteady and limp and I held on to the wall.

I was next to the dining-room window, and by putting my face close to the glass I could peer in. The table was already set for dinner, the white cloth spread out and the cutlery glinting as though nothing had happened. There was nobody in the room looking out at me, and for that I was glad, for as I moved my head away from the window my reflection sprang hideously into focus, and watching it staring dismally back at me I could see that I was not a prepossessing sight. My face was blotched with tearstains and my hair straggled tightly to the contours of my scalp. There was horror and revulsion etched on my face and a smear of vomit across my chin. I looked down and saw that below my trembling knees my shoes were also spattered with vomit.

I looked away then from myself and my reflection, and edged along the wall of the house towards the front drive, avoiding the veranda and whatever remained of the afternoon tea party. Through the churning and throbbing of my head I could vaguely discern the regular chink and murmur of normality renewed, but I knew that I could not go back and join it.

At the corner of the house I sat down again on a flat stone, and leaned against the rough brick wall. I looked down the drive to the front gate where I had once, so many endless centuries ago, met Onyango.

'Why?' I wondered again and again to myself, and occasionally 'where?' and 'how?', but the latter questions were practicalities, and it was the search and escape from reasons which saturated my shocked, aching mind, and filled my body with trembling nausea and loathing. I asked the question aloud, 'why?' once, and then again 'why?', but there was no answer from the luxuriant heat-soaked garden or from the huge empty blueness of the sky. The answers that my mind returned to me, I did not want to know about. It seemed unlikely that anyone would ever answer the question, and the issue was condemned to become another piece of furniture, probably the heaviest yet, to weigh down in the burden of guilt that I stored inside me.

My mind wandered and drifted a little, and I considered how displeased Mrs Hannett would be to know that her body was now forever bonded to the harsh soil of East Africa, and how the unlikely end that she had feared had somehow sought her out. But despite these vague wonderings I could not help returning, each time with a fresh wave of nausea, to the endless theme of why Onyango should ever have murdered the Hannetts, striking them down with his glittering machete.

Restlessness soaked into my body with the inevitable ebbing of the shock and the numbness of acceptance, resignation and guilt. I stood up, wiped clean my mouth and shoes and ran my fingers through my hair, then walked down the drive, kicking at the gravel, towards the front gate. A car was coming along the track which led past the gate into Marsdon Villas, but from the speed that it was travelling, sending up a blur of red dust and exhaust fumes, it was evidently not intending to stop or call in. I stood on the edge of the track to watch, half interested to observe the passing of this stranger. The dust cloud eddied up into my face and as I coughed and sneezed, the car glittered past before I could focus my eyes on the figures inside.

Just beyond the gateway where the track curved into a dusty bend the car slowed, stopped, and reversed to where I was standing, still spluttering in the dust and fumes. Teatime's events had so obliterated the other mysteries from my mind that I was startled to see Mr Ballantine at the wheel. He opened the door and got out, and smiled at me across the hot roof of the car. He seemed to have aged about a thousand years since I had last seen him when he had driven Ziggy, Marsdon and me down to Nairobi to take the train to Mombasa and Ocean View. His face was thin and grey and unshaven, and the pockets of tiredness in which his eyes were invariably buried had sunk into deep wells.

'Are you the send-off party?' he asked.

There was a tone of false jollity in his voice which irritated me. At least Max acted more professionally. I remembered some long-forgotten saying from Mrs O'Cavanagh in Stoney Street, 'If you can't act well, then don't bother.' Or had it been 'If you can't lie well, then don't bother'? They applied equally well to Mr Ballantine's poor performance of hearty merriment and quips. He came and stood next to me. We both leant against the car, and although we were on the shaded side, the metal was still hot to the touch.

'No. I'd forgotten that you were leaving Marsdon Villas today. Ziggy and I only arrived here this afternoon.'

Mr Ballantine nodded. He nodded slowly and for a long time, as though he was so busy thinking of something else that he had forgotten to stop.

'I'm surprised, in a way, that you came back to Marsdon Villas,' he said at last.

'Marsdon wanted Ziggy to come. I think that Arabella wanted to see him. Since Aunt Bernice died I've become quite rich; she left me everything, you see. Anyway, I paid for us both to come back here. I didn't want to stay in Cornwall on my own. I thought that . . . well . . . what I had done had been forgotten, especially after . . . what had happened here. Marsdon didn't tell us who had done it.'

'It might not have been Onyango, that's only what one witness thinks.'

'It was. They got him yesterday evening in Nairobi. He still had the machete.' I paused, and then added, 'Do you know what happened? I'd like to know.'

'I only know what everybody else knows.'

'I don't know anything. Nothing. I mean why or where or how. Nobody has told me anything at all.'

Mr Ballantine started his nodding again, then stopped. He looked anxiously up towards the house.

'OK. I'll have to be quick. They, the Hannetts that is, went into Kericho one evening, to the Tea Hotel I think, and for once in their lives they didn't take a driver. Mr Hannett drove. It seems that on the way back they had a puncture, they stopped to mend it, got out of the car and were attacked. Mr Hannett first it seems. That is it really. It was very messy I should think. It wasn't very late and Mrs Hannett's screams alerted some people who live quite near where they stopped, some of the tea-pickers actually. One of them thought that he recognized Onyango. He ran away as soon as they turned up, didn't pause to take any money or anything.'

He stopped, biting his lip as though he had said too much, and glanced down sideways at me. The look in his slanting eyes was kind, but I could tell by the way that he jiggled gently on the balls of his feet that he was in a hurry to leave.

'One more question. Please?'

He nodded and I paused and took a deep, gulping breath. This was perhaps going to be my only chance to ask anybody.

'Do you think he did it because . . . well, it was the Hannetts who came that morning . . . because . . . because of me?'

Mr Ballantine's face was serious and the hand that he put on my shoulder had all the weight of that serious expression loaded on to it.

'Onyango always hated colonials, you must know that. With no disrespect, the Hannetts did have a very colonial outlook. Some people may even have described

193

them as racist, particularly Mr Hannett actually, although his wife was much more vocal on these matters. Perhaps, and I mean just perhaps, what happened between you added to Onyango's hate for white superiority. I think, however, in fact we all think, that it would have happened anyway. He had probably come to the Highlands from his home near Lake Victoria in the hope of proving something to the British, I'm not sure what. He may easily have been seeking somebody to take his revenge on for colonialism. He found the Hannetts and the result is horrible. It might have been me. Or you. Try not to worry about it too much. It wasn't your fault.'

They were kind words I suppose, and in their way honest and fair. As he finished he straightened up, standing away from the car and pulling his shirt away from where sweat made it cling to his back and shoulders.

'Now, I had better get going. I am glad that I managed to see you, albeit briefly.'

He held out his hand to me, and I took it in a brief, formal shake. At the same time I asked, before I forgot and it was too late:

'Why are you leaving Marsdon Villas anyway?'

He gave a short humourless snort of a laugh.

'Oh. So you don't know about that either. Well, well, have a look and a guess.'

He gestured with his thumb to the back seat of the car. I bent and looked in through the closed window, my face squashed close up to the glass so that I could avoid seeing my reflection. Lolling in the back of the car, with a loose bright piece of cotton wrapped around her, was a negro woman who seemed familiar. She smiled up at my face peering anxiously and curiously in at her. It was Molly, Mr Ballantine's house servant. In her arms she cradled a fat sleeping baby. Even through the dusty half-light of the window it was clear that the baby was half-caste.

I straightened up and faced Mr Ballantine. He had walked around the car, back to the driver's door which he had half-opened, ready to get in and drive away. He laughed again at my bewildered face, a harsh, curt laugh, devoid of happiness. Then he smiled, and his smile at least was friendly and genuine.

'After all that I said to you, I still didn't learn that number one rule of not to get caught out. I've been caught and now I'm leaving with my problems. I don't want to leave, but I won't give up my problems for Max or anyone. I can't leave my problems behind, unlike you, and also unlike you I don't want to. Anyway, you can perhaps now think of me as your equal. Goodbye, Zag. Good luck and try not to worry.'

'Goodbye, Tom. Good luck.'

The car roared away in a bluster of exhaust and dust, and I raised my hand to the hands that were raised to me: Tom's and Molly's.

It was the second time that I had called Mr Ballantine Tom, and I knew that in my mind he would never be Mr Ballantine again. He was wrong when he implied that I could leave my problems behind me, for they followed me everywhere as a vanguard of guilt and regret. He was right, however, when he suggested that in some ways he had become my equal, but I could not tell whether my estimation of him had fallen or whether my estimation of myself had risen.

Chapter Thirteen

The days plopped past; succulent golden plums dropping from an unseen source. I felt as though I were a fly drowning, luxuriously, stickily, in a lake of honey into which I'd flown, as all flies do, for greed. Life continued, things moved, changed, slipped slowly over the horizon, yet nothing seemed to move or change and there seemed to be no horizons.

The Frobishers returned to Nairobi, and Marsdon and Ziggy, under Max's vociferous guidance, took over Tom's duties, while Arabella pouted and flounced, and was charming and pretty as only she knew how. Somehow, in that slow, unnoticeable way, I started to help Dr Cairns's students, Andrew and Richard, with their obscure medical research. I trailed with them around the small, squalid villages of mud and straw and scrawny chickens and thin despised yellow dogs, helping to collect data. I weighed and measured thin, ugly children with big eyes and big, bulging abdomens and arms and legs as thin, awkward and angular as the limbs of the large gawky insects that strutted sometimes across the veranda at Marsdon Villas. Some of the children had scaly, scarred skins and nearly all of them smelt of something indefinable and unpleasant. Dr Cairns said that they smelt of goats, and perhaps he was right, for those scrawny wire-haired creatures that, too rickety to gambol, mumbled around the outskirts of the villages seemed always to be tended by these children. Godfrey and Humphrey, Beatrice's children whom I had met in the kitchen of Marsdon Villas so long ago, seemed, in my memory, from an entirely different brood. I wondered if they had been scrubbed specially that day, or if they had access to facilities that these other hundreds of waif-like children, laughing and tumbling though they were, were denied.

I collected faecal samples, as I was clinically learning to call the coarse, watery, foul-smelling mushes that the children presented to me in small containers with poorly-fitting lids. I prepared these samples too, with a spatula and a small tea-strainer-like sieve, for Andrew and Richard to examine. It was tedious, tiring, unpleasant work, and the smell of it seemed to hang around me in an almost visible haze that could only be removed by a thorough bath, but it kept my body occupied. My mind, meanwhile, ran again and again along the same scared, guilty tracks and the same crooked, bitter paths leading to the horrible destiny that one day, and it could be now, Ziggy would decide that he could never forgive me.

I really felt that Max and Lily, by some curious force of willpower and determination, had managed entirely to forget what had occurred between Onyango and me. They treated me with a friendly indifference that seemed untouched by animosity, and they appeared unaware that I might quail and shudder when they mentioned him. Although they refrained in front of Arabella from the endless debate of why Onyango might have so messily slaughtered the Hannetts, they had no such compunction with me, and none of their theories included any mention of my brief affair with the murderer. Of course, they may have discussed the possibility of my sad, ridiculous part in my absence, while I was accompanying Andrew and Richard around the endless throngs of villages, but I doubt it; my fleeting incident with him had simply ceased to exist in their memories.

Once, at teatime, while everybody was gathered around on the white wicker chairs and Arabella was

197

for some reason briefly inside, Max took it upon himself to explain to me that Onyango had once been a gardener at Marsdon Villas. To my startled gaze, nobody looked incredulous at Max's unnecessary elucidation of Onyango's past, except perhaps for me, for Max had slapped me on the shoulder in his hearty military way, and roared.

'Don't look so worried, Zag dear, he's not here any more. He's safely locked up in Nairobi awaiting trial!'

Only Dr Cairns seemed to express any sign that Max's behaviour was odd, for he coughed his sharp guttural cough that he had brought all the way from Glasgow, and glared ferociously at Max across the red bristle of his moustache. Even Ziggy stared coolly and calmly ahead, and I felt that like Alice in Wonderland I had tumbled headfirst into a world so bizarre that I would never understand it, in which I would always be nibbling at the wrong side of the mushroom, and from which I would never wake up.

Nevertheless, I knew that I would one day wake up. We were to leave Marsdon Villas and Kenya at the end of February, and the inevitable approach of this awakening I viewed with a mixture of fear, loathing and hopeful anticipation. I was terrified of being in Kenya, or more precisely Marsdon Villas, during Onyango's trial, but I was also morbidly fascinated to know what would happen. Also I half-hoped, half-feared that Ziggy would refuse to come back to Cornwall with me, but would try to stay in Kenya and make Marsdon Villas his home rather than that narrow cold house of my childhood. He was happy working with Marsdon, or rather above Marsdon, in place of Tom Ballantine as under-manager in Max's tea business, for Marsdon was inept with both figures and with people, and his bumbling was inefficient and ineffective. Then there was Ziggy's courtship of Arabella — who was also lingering in Marsdon Villas, unsure of where to go or what to do – which seemed to be flourishing. Like me, Arabella had become suddenly wealthy in her own right, and she twittered prettily and helplessly about the overnight responsibility of cash, and wondered whether, as her mother had hoped and planned, she should be travelling down to South Africa, where, as she put it, whites were still whites, and blacks were still blacks.

I was certain that Ziggy would be delighted to take the burden of decisions and finance from her, and I envied her deeply for his doting attentions. If it had been only her inheritance he was courting I would have felt happier, but it was not. She looked and acted like some enchanted, ethereal being, and Ziggy was entranced by her.

On 14 February it was Marsdon's birthday. It seemed like a sad, humourless joke that this antithesis of Cupid's dreams should be born on St Valentine's Day. Nevertheless, he had been, and Max and Lily, as apparently they had every year since his first birthday, held a massive, grand and very formal party for him in the evening. More of a banquet than a party, it was the sort of event that I associated only with the luxuriance and exaggeration of fiction, and I felt more than ever that I had somehow carelessly slid into a world that did not really exist. I stood awkwardly, gawkily in corners watching the incomprehensible glitter and swirl with a fascination that was both entranced and revulsed. I shivered into the background of the wood-panelled walls, but I also felt the desperate desire to be noticed and accepted. Needless to say, when someone did speak to me I was terrified, and desperate to be ignored again.

Swarms of unknown people floated about the house on the warm February evening air, drinking, chattering, laughing. They seemed to have congregated from all over East Africa, from all over the world, but apparently most of them were usually to be found buried somewhere in Nairobi. They had taken all the rooms in the Kericho Tea Hotel, and they moaned and praised it incessantly. Things never seem to be how they once were, and the past always seems to have been better.

Every house servant was squeezed into their white-starched, braid and buttons uniforms, and they rose, or perhaps sank, to the occasion in terms of their deference and obsequiousness. Amongst the servants, the guests, all white without a drop of Asian, Oriental, or, of course, African blood in them, glowed and strutted like prize poultry, the analogy accentuated by their crowing voices which were loud and became louder.

Arabella was squeezed and petted, pecked and ruffled by such a host of stout, sweaty men and such a drooping trail of pretty, petulant wives that if she had not been so perfect in her role as the tragic orphan, I would have felt sorry for her. For Marsdon, however, my pity was not suffocated by jealousy or cynicism, for as he was by his very presence the party's *raison d'être* and therefore host, he was greeted by everybody, and then bitingly and cuttingly ignored as each of the guests scurried off to find someone more exciting and interesting to talk to. Marsdon seemed aware of this, and, squeezed into a suit that was too small for him, he was red with mortification. His conversations became increasingly beset by his stammer and his words became more and more frequently caught behind his buck teeth, finally emerging with a whistle and a distressingly obvious tail of spittle. I wondered if he had been more elegant and more an object of interest when he was only a babe at his birthday parties. Somehow, however, I imagined he had been like the Marsdon that he still was from birth.

I wished that I could escape from this bustle of food

and drink and smoke and inane, shrieking conversation to the kitchen, which, however busy, would still have that air of reality, and the calm solidity of Florence. I knew, however, and the house servants knew too, that my days of familiarity with them were long since over.

It was almost midnight and the party was in full swing, the feasting finished and Marsdon's bumbled and mercifully brief speech of gratitude performed. The throng gathered to crow and preen and cluck in the drawing room with yet more drinks and the thick furry taste of cigar smoke hanging densely in the air. I trembled in the doorway for perhaps a few minutes, undecided whether to try yet again to participate in this society that I feared but wanted. Not understanding it, I sneered at it, and it, neither fearing nor wanting me, did not understand me either, and also sneered at me.

The sneer, for it was obvious in an insidious, cold-shouldered way, decided me, and I left the doorway and crept up the wide wooden staircase, past the blankly staring animal heads on the landing walls, to my room. A small and temporary respite from the hypocritical expatriate whirl of socializing and the hectic, incomprehensible world of Marsdon Villas.

The lights were off in my room, but a gentle glow from the full moon shone demurely across the floor and walls. I walked to the window and leant my forehead against the glass. The night-time garden seemed bathed in the tranquillity of moonlight and every shrub suffused with a white glow of purity. I could feel the dark, muddled bitterness of my soul slinking into me as though ashamed by the starkness of the contrast. Such moonlight reminded me not of madness, the lunacy with which it is associated, but the guileless rectitude of clarity and perfection.

I looked out of the window across the garden for several minutes, recalling yet again the first time, so many hundreds of years ago, that I had seen Onyango. I remembered how he and Char-les had swept their machetes with clean, easy sweeps through the tangle of trailing branches. The machetes glittered in my memory with a bright and evil sharpness. Nameless negroes working the garden they had been then, Charles and Onyango, and despite everything I was still not sure that I regretted that things had not stayed that way.

I do not know how long I had been standing leaning against the window, when I was disturbed from my predictable and melancholy thought-pattern by a gentle tap at the door. I half-turned, standing back from the window a little, but not moving away from it.

'Yes. Come in.'

It was Ziggy. The light from the landing shone down on his face. He looked flushed, as though with pleasure, or more probably alcohol. His eyes shone like the glass eyes of the stuffed animal heads behind him. He smiled at me across the room as though he was delighted to see me. His smile was so genuinely warm and welcoming that I glanced quickly sideways to check that some other person had not crept un-noticed into the room while I had been dreaming out at the garden. Since we had left Ocean View he had not smiled at me like that. He clicked the door shut behind him, and strode into the room.

'Zag! I have come to make an announcement to you concerning an event of paramount importance.'

He brandished the words at me as though they were a weapon, not of defence or attack, but a theatrical prop. I smiled at his pomposity, and he laughed happily too. He came over and stood beside me at the window and looked out across the garden. He was silent for a moment, the flood of white moonlight swamping his announcements and pro-nouncements.

'It's beautiful.'

The words flickered out of him, scarcely louder than his breathing.

'It's like a mystical and unknown land.'

This was not the sort of thing that I expected Ziggy to say. Romantic description had never been one of his indulgences previously, at least not to my knowledge, and I wondered vaguely how much he had had to drink. There was certainly plenty of alcohol downstairs to float the meagre shards of communication upon.

'It's a full moon,' I said, flatly and prosaically, perhaps subconsciously attempting to be a sobering influence. Ziggy laughed, a low gurgling laugh, and I knew that he was laughing at me, but not maliciously.

'Zag, you are so practical. Look at the unearthly beauty of it. I would have thought you would have loved it. It is the very web that dreams are spun from. You'll be telling me that you don't believe in fairies next.'

'I don't believe in fairies.'

His laugh again was low and gurgling, rising from somewhere deep inside him. It was a happy, friendly sound, and it seemed as though all the bitter rancour that had snarled around us since Ocean View had suddenly and completely vanished, evaporated by the purity of the moonbeams. I laughed too then, full of hope, but my laugh stopped short in mid-cadence. I knew that this happiness between us was only a dream spun on a fragile web, only a facet of alcohol, only a trick of the moonlight.

'That was a very abrupt laugh,' said Ziggy gently.

His voice sank a little so that I had to lean forward to catch his words. He spoke very seriously.

'I didn't realize how beautiful you had grown of late, little Zag.'

I didn't know how to answer that, and I looked up at him fearfully. We were standing very close together by

203

the window, his left arm so near my right that I could feel the golden hairs on it brushing my skin. He bent his head, bringing his face down towards mine. Closer and closer his face came, like an enormous moon. His eyes looked directly into mine, and I felt that our gazes were bound to each other on unbreakable silver cords. With a clutch of fear, exhilaration and helplessness I knew what was going to happen even before our lips touched.

Later, much later in terms of pleasure, experience and, I suppose by some people's reckoning, sin, and not so very much later in terms of that prosaic measure called time, we lay together on the bed. Our naked limbs were entwined and our naked bodies seemed soldered together by the sweet stickiness of sweat and shared ecstasy.

'You are the first white person that I have ever made love to,' murmured Ziggy. His lips were so close that I could feel them flickering past my ear, fluttering the small damp tendrils of my hair that hung there. I was silent for just a few gentle, precious moments.

'You are the first white person that I have ever made love to, as well,' I replied, also very softly.

My words had broken the spell however, fading the moonlight out of the room and bringing our web of fairyland back down to the hypocrisy and half-truths of Marsdon Villas. We seemed to realize this simultaneously, as though we were still partially in harmony. Our bodies fell apart wordlessly and before long we were dressed again and ready to return to the unknowing party downstairs. I broke the silence before we left the room, afraid that otherwise a new wall of guilt and regret might build up between us.

'So what important announcement did you come to proclaim to me?'

'Oh, of course! I nearly forgot!'

I was glad that his laugh was full of pleasure and humour and that I could hear no echoes of remorse.

'I asked her and she said yes. Arabella and I are going to get married. We want you and Marsdon to be bridesmaid and best man.'

THE END

Shining Agnes
by Sara Banerji

'A delightful tale . . . blackly comic'
Philippa Logan, *Oxford Times*

In a once great, now falling, mansion live an aristocratic
family: Alice, huge, sad and longing for love; her
paralysed mother who is subject to wild and eccentric
enthusiasms; and the foster child Agnes, whose desire to
be an actress sets in motion a train of bizarre and
horrifying events.

Then love comes to Alice in the form of the beautiful but
furtive Vincent who has moved in next door. But does he
want Alice for herself or for the treasure that she digs from
the rubble of her tumbled home? And how does he view
Alice's obsession with compost, the making of which she
compares to the growth of spirituality and the purging
away of sin?

Black comedy lurks beneath the surface of this gloriously
imaginative new novel from the author of
Cobwebwalking, The Wedding of Jayanthi Mandel and
The Tea-Planter's Daughter.

'A novel as robust and muscular as Alice herself, and as
rich, dark and fertile as her compost'
Christopher Potter, *The Listener*

'Banerji's writing has the darkness of Muriel Spark and
the grace of Alice Thomas Ellis'
Clare Boylan, *Sunday Times*

0 552 99459 6

BLACK SWAN

Vermin Blond
by Richard Davis

'Everyone called him Gaby. To have known him meant to be uneasy ever after . . .'

Why should a middle-aged solicitor abandon his wife, his home and his job, to dispose of a dead friend's estate? To find the answer Mark Palfreyman must delve into his past and confront its demons.

He looks back to 1968 and his last year at St Clement's, a boys' public boarding school, and the people who dominated his adolescence: his family, well-meaning but an embarrassment; Ambrose, the crushingly rude senior tutor; Judy, the history master's girlfriend and Mark's 'Ideal Woman'. But looming over them all is Martin Gabriel – Gaby – the rebel angel who dazzles man and woman, master and pupil alike. Mark, too, is captivated, but as he is drawn into Gaby's select circle, he glimpses a darker, grimmer side to the 'vermin blond' charmer.

VERMIN BLOND brilliantly captures the claustrophobic atmosphere of an all-male society. Its savage denouement is at once believable and shocking.

'I was impressed by the assured authorial voice, and completely gripped by the characters throughout'
Robert Carver, *Observer*

'Davis knows his patch well and acutely observes the tribal alliances, cold-shower ethics and repressed sexuality of this warping environment'
Nicholas Marston, *GQ*

0 552 99484 7

BLACK SWAN

A SELECTION OF FINE WRITING FROM BLACK SWAN

THE PRICES SHOWN BELOW WERE CORRECT AT THE TIME OF GOING TO PRESS. HOWEVER TRANSWORLD PUBLISHERS RESERVE THE RIGHT TO SHOW NEW RETAIL PRICES ON COVERS WHICH MAY DIFFER FROM THOSE PREVIOUSLY ADVERTISED IN THE TEXT OR ELSEWHERE.

☐ 99198 8	THE HOUSE OF THE SPIRITS	*Isabel Allende*	£5.99
☐ 99313 1	OF LOVE AND SHADOWS	*Isabel Allende*	£5.99
☐ 99248 8	THE DONE THING	*Patricia Angadi*	£4.99
☐ 99201 1	THE GOVERNESS	*Patricia Angadi*	£3.99
☐ 99322 0	THE HIGHLY FAVOURED LADIES	*Patricia Angadi*	£3.99
☐ 99464 2	PLAYING FOR REAL	*Patricia Angadi*	£4.99
☐ 99385 9	SINS OF THE MOTHERS	*Patricia Angadi*	£3.99
☐ 99459 6	SHINING AGNES	*Sara Banerji*	£4.99
☐ 99186 4	A KIND OF LOVING	*Stan Barstow*	£4.99
☐ 99434 0	GIVE US THIS DAY	*Stan Barstow*	£4.99
☐ 99176 7	JOBY	*Stan Barstow*	£3.50
☐ 99484 7	VERMIN BLOND	*Richard Davis*	£4.99
☐ 99449 9	DISAPPEARING ACTS	*Terry McMillan*	£4.99
☐ 99480 4	MAMA	*Terry McMillan*	£4.99
☐ 99056 6	BROTHER OF THE MORE FAMOUS JACK	*Barbara Trapido*	£4.99
☐ 99130 9	NOAH'S ARK	*Barbara Trapido*	£4.99
☐ 99126 0	THE CAMOMILE LAWN	*Mary Wesley*	£5.99
☐ 99210 0	HARNESSING PEACOCKS	*Mary Wesley*	£4.99
☐ 99082 5	JUMPING THE QUEUE	*Mary Wesley*	£4.99
☐ 99304 2	NOT THAT SORT OF GIRL	*Mary Wesley*	£4.99
☐ 99355 7	SECOND FIDDLE	*Mary Wesley*	£4.99
☐ 99393 X	A SENSIBLE LIFE	*Mary Wesley*	£5.99
☐ 99258 5	THE VACILLATIONS OF POPPY CAREW	*Mary Wesley*	£5.99

All Black Swan Books are available at your bookshop or newsagent, or can be ordered from the following address:

Corgi/Bantam Books,
Cash Sales Department
P.O. Box 11, Falmouth, Cornwall TR10 9EN

UK and B.F.P.O. customers please send a cheque or postal order (no currency) and allow £1.00 for postage and packing for the first book plus 50p for the second book and 30p for each additional book to a maximum charge of £3.00 (7 books plus).

Overseas customers, including Eire, please allow £2.00 for postage and packing for the first book plus £1.00 for the second book and 50p for each subsequent title ordered.

NAME (Block Letters) ....

ADDRESS ....

....